Tracy,
Hope you bro
your assette
C V H

WE DID EVERYTHING WRONG

C.V. Hunt

ATLATL
DAYTON, OHIO

Atlatl Press
POB 293161
Dayton, Ohio 45429
www.atlatlpress.com

WE
DID
EVERTHING
WRONG

To Andy,

You'll always be the Waldorf to my Statler.

I

The stewardess had a callus on the knuckle of her middle finger. The prominent one when you make a fist. It was a callus you saw on a fighter's hand and it was out of place on a stewardess.

She appeared to be in her forties or possibly fifties. When you got to be my age it was hard to tell someone else's, especially if they were younger. Twelve-year-old girls wore racy outfits and were mature beyond their age: smoking, drinking, fucking. Forty-year-old men lived in their parents' basement, played computer games all day, didn't work, and were given an allowance from said parents. How could anyone guess another person's actual age anymore? Age was literally just a measurement. It didn't correspond to any kind of life arc.

At sixty-five my life had flown by in a blur. I knew it could all come to a screeching halt at any moment. And I was no longer sure if I was okay with that or not. Rewind to a couple of weeks ago I could've given you a definitive answer. I was ready to go. There wasn't anything left. I wouldn't leave much behind. I hadn't accomplished much. And I didn't know the meaning of life any more now than I did when everything went from bad to worse.

The stewardess leisurely made her way down the aisle of the aircraft. She gripped the headrests to steady herself as the plane bucked with the turbulence. I couldn't help but wonder what caused the callus on her knuckle. Was she so frustrated with her life that once she landed and clocked out and was past the terminals and the security check points and the cabs and the rental cars and the parking lot full of temporarily abandoned cars and the highways full of construction and the self-involved people paying more attention to the last text they received or the text they were about to send or the phone call they were attending to and past the copycat suburbs and shitty school systems and the decrepit hospitals and everything else her hard earned tax dollars paid for that she pulled into her driveway and dragged herself up the walkway and into her house and kicked off her shoes and walked up her stairs to her affordably decorated IKEA bedroom with the funky pattern duvet cover she had to have where she repeatedly punched some inanimate object and cried to let out all of the disappointment and frustrations of her life and let the punches melt into a staccato of nothingness until she was exhausted and it all felt meaningless before crawling into her lonely bed with a sore hand and tears drying on her cheeks as she drifted off into the sweet release of sleep? I wanted to think that was *exactly* what she did. I didn't want to think the callus was from kneading bread or another rational loving act. It made me feel less alone to think she was a fighter. It made me feel good I wasn't alone in the never-ending soft nightmare everyone calls life.

The aisle seat was claustrophobic. The woman sandwiched between me and the man in the window seat was extremely overweight. She fidgeted for the millionth time and elbowed me in the bicep. I took a deep breath and let it out slowly and told myself I was almost home and not to belittle the woman about her blatant disregard for her fellow human beings' comfort. I only had to endure this for a few more minutes. I pulled my shoulders together, tighter than before, and hoped she didn't touch me again. The woman didn't appear to be hygienic. Her face was greasy. She emanated an odor of unwashed skin and cigarette smoke. Her shirt was stained and torn and adorned with speckled bleach spots. She wore pink fuzzy pajama pants and those awful shoes that were all the rage five or ten years ago. What were they called? They were named after an animal.

The stewardess laid her hand on the headrest in front of me and stopped. She asked the overweight woman to put her seat in the upright position for landing. The woman grappled with the button on the armrest separating us and somehow managed to elbow me in the ribs a couple of times. I closed my eyes and bit back the urge to tell her an apology for bruising the fuck out of my side would be nice.

This should not be happening. I should've been dead less than a week ago.

Crocs. Her stupid and ugly shoes were called Crocs. Why did my memory work this way after all these years?

I opened my eyes and the stewardess was gone. I stared aimlessly in the direction of the fat woman's shoes but all I could make out now was an abundance of fuzzy pink fat thighs. I wondered when air travel became like this. I hadn't traveled by plane a lot in my lifetime but I do remember a time when there was plenty of space between the aisle and the seats were much bigger and men and women would wear their Sunday best and the armrest housed an ashtray instead of buttons to control a television mounted into the back of every seat because society couldn't go a few hours without being entertained by brainless television programming. Forget reading a book. Forget trying to have a normal conversation with the person sitting next to you. Forget dressing up and boarding a plane and chain-smoking and drinking highballs like you were on a party craft ten thousand feet in the air. Now smoking was bad and you were viewed as some sort of demon if you subjected anyone within viewing distance to the presence of your addiction. There wasn't time to dress up. And the art of conversation died the day the Internet was invented. You couldn't even make eye contact with someone these days without them becoming nervous and shifty and reaching for a prescription bottle to calm their panic attack or soothe their ADHD or whatever Internet search self-diagnosed disorder they had. People weren't civil to one another anymore.

The captain made his final announcement and notified the flight attendants they should return to their seats for landing.

Flight attendants.

I cringed.

In my mind I referred to the woman with the callused knuckle as a stewardess. I used a term now considered politically incorrect. When was it all going to end? When would enough be enough? When was everyone going to get their ribbon for participation? Why couldn't this god damn plane dive nose-first into the tarmac and put us all out of our misery?

And I wouldn't be on this damn plane full of brainlessness and rudeness if it weren't for Horace. Why did he have to interrupt me? Why did I answer him? When was this all really going to end? I was so close. Maybe I'm close now.

2

I stood in front of the bathroom vanity and reread the warning label on the prescription bottle of sleeping pills. It hadn't been as hard as what I thought it would be to acquire them. A trip to my local doctor in the small town where I lived, a complaint of numerous sleepless nights, add the sad-sap story about Beverly dying nine months ago, and voilà, an endless prescription and a kickback to the doctor for prescribing it. No one wanted to actually help anyone anymore. They wanted to give you a pill so you would go away. The more pills they prescribed the more money they made. And hell, why not give people what they asked for? The doctors made more money giving people what they wanted instead of what they actually needed. This would keep them coming back and paying the copay and asking for more pills and tests and whatever other money sucking item they could think of because they'd searched for their symptoms online and diagnosed themselves without years of medical schooling and a degree. The customer was always right.

I poured out a handful of the tiny white oblong pills. I bounced them in my palm and filled a glass from the tap.

The old rotary plastic phone rang in my office, startling me. I jerked from the fright and splashed some of the water on the crotch of my pants. I cursed under my breath. My pants might not be dry by the time someone found me. What did it matter? I'd heard people shit their pants when they die. A wet spot on my favorite dress pants would be the least worry for the person who found me. Unless the person was like all the other assholes in the world nowadays.

An image flashed in my mind of a twenty-something taking photos of me dead, in my bed, with a wet spot on my crotch. The little shit would upload it to the Internet for all of his asshole buddies to see. His buddies, in return, would write a quip under the photo along the lines of 'look at this old dude who pissed his pants when he died'. The sentence they wrote would be full of typos and all his friends would laugh and leave degrading remarks confirming how clever their friend was but in actuality they'd never met the smartass before.

The phone rang a second time. I laid the handful of pills on the counter and grabbed the fluffy pink hand towel from the wall rack. I dabbed my crotch and tried to dry the water. I tried not to think about how Beverly specifically picked out this ugly towel for the bathroom even though she knew I hated pink.

The phone rang a third time. I threw the towel on the counter and scooped up the pills.

The sound of the phone had grown grating the last nine months. After Beverly died the phone didn't stop ringing for a week and half. It rang at three in the afternoon and three in the morning: people from the local church, family, friends, old high school acquaintances, a former coworker from twenty years ago, the kids' friends from elementary school. Then, as suddenly as her death happened, the phone stopped.

The phone rang again and I cringed.

My house became ground zero for sorrow shortly after Beverly's death. I didn't have time to grieve properly with my son and his wife around all the time, along with my daughter and her two brats. I didn't know from one ring to the next whether it would be an emotional and personal call or a work related telephone conversation—a disadvantage of working from home.

The phone shrilled and I knew it would be the final time. I wasn't going to answer it. The decrepit answering machine would take a message.

I inspected my age-lined face and thinning gray hair in the mirror as the click and the tape reel of the answering machine kicked in. Beverly's voice emanated from my office as she announced to the caller they had reached the Koyfman residence and we were unable to answer the phone and to leave their name and number so we could return their call. I remembered how Beverly made it a point to say we were unable to answer the phone and not that we weren't home because someone might take the opportunity to rob us. I remembered standing in the office with her and telling her if you didn't answer the phone any intelligent person would know you weren't home. And of the people who called, who would rob us? Family? Friends? The remark stung Beverly and I remembered the tiny and nearly indecipherable change in her face when I'd made the statement. Recalling her face from that moment sent a pain through my gut like someone had punched me. How had I managed to keep her all those years when I constantly acted like a shithead? But still, the thought was ludicrous to add such a statement to the answering machine. In the end I nodded when she asked if the message sounded okay. It was always best to let her have her way. I never could stand to see her upset.

A sob rose in my chest and I choked it back. My eyes watered and I blinked rapidly. I stared at my reflection and inspected the dark circles under my eyes. I weighed the pills in my hand and checked the bottle to see how many were left.

Horace's distorted voice blared through the tiny speaker of the answering machine. "Aaaabe! Abraham!" There was a brief pause and he slurred, "I can't believe you haven't changed that message." He breathed heavily and came back authoritative. "Abraham, this is Dr. Sherwin. Answer your phone." Another pause. "I know you're there. Answer the phone. I'm in the area and I'm stopping by."

I forced the pills back into the bottle, dropping some on the floor.

Horace said, "I'm going to break into your house and shit on your desk if you're not there."

I dodged into the office and snatched up the phone. The answering machine emanated a series of high pitched squeals before I could hit the stop button. I held the phone to my ear. Horace shouted something unintelligible and told someone in the background he would plow their cunt again as soon as he was off the phone.

I said, "Horace."

"Heeeey," he slurred.

"You're drunk. It's . . ." The clock on my desk displayed 11:32. "It's not even noon."

He shouted, "Who cares?!"

I pulled the phone away from my ear. "You don't have to shout."

"I'm not shouting!"

"Yes you are."

"I'm in town. I'm going to stop by."

"I'm busy."

"No you're not. You're never busy. You work from home."

"I'm still—"

"Selling cassette tapes! Are you still selling those brainwashing Zig Ziglar pieces of shit?" He laughed.

"It's not Zig Ziglar. They're Dr. Wiwi's subliminal self-help tapes."

Horace burst into a fit of laughter. He tried to repeat Dr. Wiwi's name in between laughs but this sent him into another round of hysterics.

I shouted, "Don't you have anything better to do!"

He quieted himself. "I'm retired. I spend my time banging broads!" Someone reprimanded him in the background and he told them to shut up. "You should be banging broads too. How long has it been since you got laid?"

"I don—"

"Jesus Christ! Beverly's been dead forever!"

I clipped, "It's only been nine months."

"That's long enough!"

"Fuck you, Horace!"

He shouted he was on his way over as I slammed the receiver down. I grabbed the cord for the phone connecting it to the wall and ripped it out. I snatched the phone off the desk, lifted it above my head, and threw it down on the floor as hard as I could. The bell inside gave a sharp ring on contact. The mouth piece popped free of the receiver, clattering across the floor. The clear rotary number wheel bounced off my desk and broke. I sat down at my desk and began to sob.

Nine months. Nine *long* months of aimlessness and loneliness and sleeplessness and hurt and depression and wanting it all to end or get better. I knew at this point it was never going to get better. When you looked at the scope of life it took nine months to be born. It was appropriate for it to take nine months to die.

Not for Beverly though. She didn't get nine months. She sat across from me one Thursday morning eating breakfast, looking at a sale flyer. She made a comment on how expensive steaks were. To this day I still try to remember her exact words. They were so banal and throw away and it makes me sad to think they were her last. Suddenly she looked at me confused and her hand holding the flyer began to tremble. My mouth was full of food and I was about to ask her if something was wrong. But her expression shifted to terror before I could swallow my food. Her whole body convulsed violently and she fell forward into her bowl of oatmeal. The doctor told me even if she would have been in a hospital and surrounded by doctors at the time her chances would've been slim. An aortic aneurysm. It was quick. Here one minute and gone without a chance the next.

The look of terror on her face before she collapsed was seared into my brain forever. Her exact last words I could never remember but her face would never go away no matter how much I tried. It was the expression I imagined a person would make when they looked death straight in the face and knew there was no hope.

I wiped the tears from my face with the back of my hand. For half a minute I thought about running into the bathroom, snatching up all the pills, and downing them before Horace showed up. That would show him. I should have ignored the phone, downed them, and went to bed. But I worried they wouldn't work before he showed up. He'd said he was in town. I lived in a small town of about five thousand people. It was a touristy place in the Midwest. People frequently visited the town on the weekend to eat overpriced and subpar food or buy trinkets the local hippies made or drink at one of the three bars or the brewery. If Horace was in town it meant he would be here within the next ten minutes. I wasn't an expert on suicide by prescription sleeping medication but I didn't think it would work quickly. And the last thing I wanted was for Horace to show up, find what I'd done, and call the police. The last thing I wanted was to have my stomach pumped and be admitted for a psychiatric evaluation. What I did want was my death on my terms and no interruptions.

I stood and proceeded to clean up the broken pieces of the telephone. I dumped the fragments of demolished plastic into the waste can I kept under my desk. When I was finished I proceeded back to the bathroom. A few of the sleeping pills lay on the floor. I retrieved the spilled tablets and poured them back into the bottle. I stared at the bottle for a few seconds before I put it back in the medicine cabinet. After all, there was tomorrow, and after a visit from Horace I was sure to be ready.

3

The sound of two car doors shutting prompted me to peek out the kitchen window. Horace and a short, haggard woman stumbled from Horace's car and under the carport attached to the house where I kept my car parked. The two clumsily made their way to the second door under the carport. It was apparent they were both inebriated.

The woman wore clothing more suited for a thirteen-year-old street walker. Her low-cut shirt was screened with the image of a female popstar making an idiotic face. The shirt was too tight and the length wasn't long enough to cover her large paunch of a stomach covered in stretch marks. Her large breasts sagged and threatened to fall below the hem of her shirt. At first I didn't think she was wearing pants until she turned sideways and stumbled into Horace, attempting to give him a sloppy kiss. It was then I realized her gut covered the front of a miniskirt.

Horace was dressed in his usual attire: a plain T-shirt,

jeans, and too many necklaces and rings for a man. I didn't understand why he wore all those accessories in the nineties until I realized what my son and daughter were wearing around the same time. Then it made sense. Horace was a trend hopper but I think the nineties was his last stop. All those necklaces and rings were fashionable then. Each piece of jewelry was engraved or painted with some type of Asian character that stood for enlightenment or strength or something the wearer was hoping to achieve by wearing it daily but all they ever got was a patch of green skin from the cheap metal. My kids grew out of the trend. Horace never did.

I strolled into the dining room and opened the door before either of them could knock. Horace was pawing through my mail. The box was located by the door and he always snooped through my belongings. His expression was that of a child caught doing something they'd been told a hundred times not to.

The woman beside him appeared as though she'd slept in her makeup. Her eyeliner was smudged and irregular and her eyelids drooped as if she were high. She leaned forward, smiled broadly, and giggled.

Horace shoved the handful of mail at me. "Hey, Abe!"

I took a few steps back and dropped the mail on the dining room table. The couple took my retreat from the doorway as an invitation to enter and barged in.

Horace snatched me up in a bear hug and slapped my back. "It's been forever! How the fuck have you been?" He let go of me and stepped back.

"My wife died. How do think I've been?"

The woman laughed. I glared at her and hoped it made her uncomfortable. She continued to grin in an idiotic fashion and was either unaware or didn't care that I didn't approve of her.

Horace said, "We're not gonna talk about it. Come on! I stopped by to see you and to have a good time. Nobody's having a good time talking about dead people!"

"You don't have to shout," I said.

"I'm not shouting!"

He stepped past me and into the kitchen. The woman closed her eyes, stumbled, and laughed. I left her to figure out what to do with herself and followed Horace.

He opened the Frigidaire and peered inside. "Jesus Christ this is depressing! Where's the beer?!"

"I don't have any beer. I can't dri—"

"What do ya mean you don't have any beer? Look at this!" He waved his hand at the open Frigidaire. "You don't have any food either. All you have is ketchup! This is the most depressing thing I've ever seen!"

"I'm too depressed to drink."

The woman laughed directly behind me. I started at the sound of her. I hadn't noticed she'd followed me. Horace slammed the icebox door.

"Too depressed?" Horace said. "Drinking was invented by depressed people! What do you think the Neanderthals did in their spare time? All they did was run around with no clothes and shit in the river and hunt beasts to eat. Does that sound fun? No! They were like this shit is depressing and I need a beer!"

The woman laughed and said, "It sounds fun to me. I'd like to run around naked." She threw her arms above her head and began to dance in what she thought was a seductive manner. I was more worried about the hem of her shirt rising too much and her breasts becoming exposed.

"Shut up, Carol!" Horace shouted. "You're gross! Make yourself useful and disappear. Was I talking to you? If I was talking to you I would have addressed you. Jesus, you're fucking disgusting!"

Carol laughed as if she thought Horace's insults were a joke. I'd known Horace long enough to know he was dead serious. Carol closed her eyes and smiled in a cat-like manner before she turned and sauntered into the living room.

I pointed in her direction after she was gone. "Are you fucking serious?"

Horace leaned against the kitchen counter. "We've been up all night snorting Adderall. Have you ever snorted Adderall? Do you know what it is?"

"No. I mean I know what Adder—"

"It's similar to doing cocaine but it's not as good. Carol has a lot of Adderall. Do you want to snort some? She's got an attention problem or something."

"No. I don't want to snort Adderall."

"We should go get some beer."

"Can we just visit for a bit? I'm not really in the mood to drink. It's too early."

"It's not too early! It's too late! I haven't been to bed yet. We should go to the bar."

"It's barely past noon. Most of the places in town don't open until three. We'll wait until supper time—"

"I'll be sober by then!" He pulled a smashed pack of cigarettes from his pants pocket and placed a bent cigarette between his lips.

"You can't smoke in here."

He pulled the smoke from his mouth. "Why not?!" He tapped me on the shoulder with his cigarette holding hand.

"You own this place, right? You don't rent. You can do whatever you want!"

I sighed and pinched the bridge of my nose. "Because I don't want my house smelling like an ashtray. If you want to smoke you have to go outside."

He grumbled and tried to shove the damaged cigarette back into the pack but ended up breaking it. He threw it in the kitchen garbage angrily and sloppily shoved the pack back into his pocket, possibly destroying the remaining cigarettes.

Dealing with Horace was frustrating. He was loud and overbearing and disagreeable and always talked overtop of you . . . and that was when he was sober. He was a thousand times worse when he was drunk.

I said, "How about I make some coffee?"

"How about I drive to the gas station and buy some more beer?"

He retrieved his car keys from his front pants pocket and jangled them. I took advantage of his intoxicated state and snatched them from his hand.

"Hey!" he shouted and tried to grab the keys.

I shoved the keys into my own pocket. "You're too drunk to be driving. You shouldn't have driven *here*. Besides, I told you I'm not in the mood to drink."

"I paid for that car! I can drive it whenever I want."

Horace lunged at me, grappled with me, and tried to put me in a headlock. I twisted out of his grasp. He tried to grab me again. I sidestepped him and he fell to the floor. He screamed when he hit the floor, rolled over, and looked at me, wounded.

"Quit acting like a child," I said.

He laughed. "Help! I've fallen and I can't get up!"

"Cliché," I said, "but more your age. Did you break a hip?"

It took him some effort to get to his feet. Once he was upright he stumbled into the living room and began to berate Carol. I ignored them and made a pot of coffee. They talked loudly about each other's physical faults and fell silent after a while.

I assumed they might have fallen asleep or passed out. Then my parental instinct kicked in. Whenever the house grew quiet when the kids were small there was no doubt I would find them doing something they knew they shouldn't. I didn't know what the relationship was between Horace and Carol but it didn't take a rocket scientist to figure it out. And Horace wasn't a bashful person. He'd performed some questionable acts within eyeshot of me on multiple occasions. Carol didn't seem to be a modest person either. I peeked around the corner to make sure they weren't having intercourse on my furniture, or snorting Adderall off the coffee table, or god knows what.

Carol was posed on the sofa in a suggestive manner. Her arm was extended above her head, cell phone in hand. She kept making bedroom eyes at the phone and licking her lips and pulling the neckline of her shirt down to show more of her sagging and age-spotted cleavage. The phone occasionally made the soft, artificial noise a camera made when you snapped a photo.

Horace sat in one of the chairs beside the sofa, sliding his thumb over the front of his phone and staring at it intently. I wasn't sure if he was intentionally ignoring Carol or if he was more interested in the electronic device.

When the coffee was done I poured two cups and entered the living room. I sat one cup on the coffee table and tapped Horace on the shoulder to get his attention. He barely pried his eyes from his phone and took the cup from me.

I sat in the recliner and watched both of them.

Carol glanced at her coffee and said, "I don't drink coffee."

Horace's phone suddenly emanated the unmistakable moans of a woman having sex. The moan was accompanied with wet sounds of flesh on flesh.

"God damn it," I said. "Are you watching porn on that thing?"

Without looking up he said, "Have you ever watched choose your own adventure porn?"

"No," I said indignantly.

Carol reached inside her shirt and pulled her breast up to expose one of her large and misshaped nipples. She snapped another photo and said, "Prude," before tucking her breast back into her shirt.

I said, "I'm not a prude."

Horace's phone continued to make sexual sounds. He stood and strode toward me. "You have to see this."

"I don't want to see it." I waved my hand dismissively at him.

He ignored me. Or rather didn't see my animated gesture because his eyes were still locked on the scene playing on his phone. He plopped his ass down on the arm of the recliner and threatened to tip the chair over. He shoved his phone in my face. I wasn't sure if it was because the grandkids did this to me all the time with their brainless shows and Internet videos that caused his actions to enrage me or if it was because I personally believed viewing pornography was a private event. I smacked his hand holding the phone and he dropped the device in my lap. Squeals of pleasure sounded from my crotch as the video continued to play and Horace groped for his phone haphazardly, fondling my dick in the process.

"Stop touching my penis!" I shouted.

Carol burst into a fit of laughter and began taking photos of the conflict. I threw Horace's phone on the floor and pushed him off the chair. He stumbled but caught himself before he fell and retrieved his phone. Carol continued to laugh and had difficultly catching her breath.

"Shut up!" Horace yelled and fiddled with his phone until it stopped making noise.

Carol sprawled out on the sofa as if she were some ancient royalty awaiting a servant to feed her grapes.

Horace mocked her laughter. He said, "Grow up. Look at you! You're a hot fuckin' mess! How old are you anyway? Taking pictures of your shitty, saggy tits. No one wants to see that shit! You know who wants to see those nasty gross breasts? Forty-year-old men who still live in their parents' basement and the closest they've ever gotten to having real sex was the one time they paid for a prostitute but couldn't keep it hard because they were too scared to fuck. You're gross! I can't believe you'd think anyone would want to see you naked."

"You wanted to see me naked," she said. "You fucked me."

He shouted, "I don't have any standards! And I'm a horny old man! I'd fuck anyone who gave me a chance! I'd fuck Abe if he let me!"

I said, "I would kill you."

They both ignored me and continued their argument.

Carol said, "You'd be surprised who finds me attractive. I have Facebook, Twitter, and Tumblr. I have to post the safer photos on Facebook but I still get hundreds of likes. People think I'm hot."

"Those are pity likes," Horace said. "They see your photos and they're saying to themselves, 'Look at this gross, fat, old, grandma. How disgusting. I guess I should like it before she goes all militant feminist and accuses me of fat shaming and hangs herself.'"

"Fuck you," she retorted.

"You guys sound like my grandkids," I said. "You're speaking a language I don't understand. Likes. Facebook. Twitter. You've all gone crazy. It's as if you have a screw loose and you're spewing random words or talking in tongues."

Carol looked at me as if I'd shat on the floor. She said, "Are you fucking serious?"

"Abe has basic technology. He isn't up to par." He turned to me. "Get a cell phone yet?"

"There's no need—"

He said, "Everyone needs a cell phone!"

Carol interjected disgustedly, "Oh my god."

"When am I ever away from home?" I said. "The only time I leave the house is to go to the store, which is a ten minute walk when the weather is decent. There's a house every god damn ten feet between here and there. If I'm driving and happen to have car trouble I'm sure I can manage—"

"What if there's an emergency?" Horace said.

"What emergency? Beverly is dead. There isn't much more that can go wrong."

Carol rolled onto her stomach. She propped herself up on her elbows, smashing her breasts into an unnatural pile of flesh. She bent her knees to raise her legs and crossed her ankles. She looked like a demented and grotesque school girl. "What about your kids and grandkids?"

"I think they can manage without me," I said. "There isn't much I can do in the event of an emergency anyway since they live two hours away."

"His kids are shitheads," Horace said.

Carol laughed and turned her attention to her phone. She slid her thumb over the screen and her expression went blank. Horace lost interest in any conversation and turned his attention back to his phone also. Carol made an exasperated sound and furrowed her brows. She poked her fingers at the screen of her phone rapidly and cursed. When she was finished with whatever occupied her she dumped her phone on the coffee table unceremoniously and flopped down flat on her stomach with her head turned toward me.

She pouted. "Some people are so narrow-minded." After a beat of neither of us responding to her she sat up and said, "People on Facebook keep reporting my photos. You can't even see my nips. People are prudes."

She pulled her legs up and crossed her legs Indian style. Her actions lifted her sagging stomach and I was given what I thought was a clear shot of her black underpants. It took me a few seconds to realize I could see an obvious slit of flesh in the crotch area. She wasn't wearing underpants. What I was seeing was her massive amount of black pubic hair.

I averted my eyes and shrugged my shoulders. My response was partly because I had no clue what she was talking about and partly because I didn't care. I was ready for both of them to leave. There was nothing engaging happening in the conversation and everything the two of them were doing and talking about only reaffirmed this world no longer belonged to me or my generation. Their presence suddenly filled me with an overwhelming sadness. I felt more alone and isolated now than the moment I poured the sleeping pills into the palm of my hand. Every single human being was wrapped up in their own narcissistic universe. It made me sick to my stomach to watch these two or a stranger on the street or the couples I passed sitting in the café uptown or my grandkids, with all of their eyes glued to a phone or a laptop or some other form of electronic device, never lifting their eyes when someone spoke to them, only grunting or agreeing or making some sort of Neanderthal sound so the person trying to rouse a response from them was placated.

Horace said, "I told you no one wants to see your gross ass."

"They're my friends," she said. "If they don't like it they should unfriend me."

Horace did a double take. "Close your god damn legs! Jesus! Don't you have any fucking humility?"

She gave him a sour look. She uncrossed her legs and spread them as wide as she could and planted her feet on the floor. I kept my eyes on Horace.

He shouted, "You're gonna stink up Abe's house with your rotten pussy! Abe doesn't want his house smelling like old woman desperation!" He turned to me. "Do you Abe?"

I said, "I think both of you have overstayed your we—"

"See?" He pointed at me and turned back to her. "He wants you to leave."

She closed her legs. "I'm not going anywhere."

Horace addressed me, "Let's go to the bar. I need an-other beer. I think I'm starting to sober up."

"I told you the bar doesn't open until—"

4

The three of us were standing outside the entrance when a waitress unlocked the bar. I tried to hide my face as much as possible whenever someone passed us on the sidewalk. Between Carol's outfit and Horace's loud demeanor I was embarrassed to be seen with them. I tried to stand a few feet away and look as though I was someone who came here for the tourist destinations.

I should've known better. Horace eventually disguised his intentions and told me he wanted to walk into town to sightsee. It was a nice day but I was reluctant to agree to walk into town. I knew it was a ploy so Horace could go to the gas station and buy more beer. I fought the suggestion for a while but knew it would be easier if I gave up. Maybe it would help the day pass quicker or he would get bored or tired and decide to leave. Sometimes it was easier to let Horace do whatever he wanted or I'd hear about it for the next few hours, repeatedly, like an overgrown spoiled brat who knows if he irritates his parents enough they will cave and let him have what he wants to shut him up. So I gave up and led him uptown.

The way Horace purchased beer at the gas station depressed me even more, which didn't seem possible. He didn't shop by name brand or taste preference. He would lift the twenty-two ounce craft beer bottles, threatening to drop them, and scan the labels until he found the alcohol percentage. He scoffed at anything that didn't proudly boast nine percent or higher. He purchased two bottles and a pack of cigarettes and ducked into some overgrown hedges beside the station to chug the beer and maintain his level of drunkenness until the bar opened.

After he finished the beer we proceeded to stand outside the bar and wait for it to open. Horace chain smoked the entire time and complained there needed to be twenty-four hour bars. Carol repeatedly bummed cigarettes from Horace. I tried coaxing them into walking on the bike trails running out beyond the town limits. Maybe that way they wouldn't be a prominent annoying debacle for the police to possibly arrest for public intoxication. Horace was extremely judgmental of every person he saw and talked too loudly about their physical flaws. I imagined at any moment one of his verbal assault victims would snap and cause some sort of scuffle. His trash talking used to be a source of entertainment. But now I found it sad and mean and hypocritical for him to give his unbridled opinion of a stranger's appearance. He was a mental, emotional, and physical mess himself and had no room to judge someone else.

A girl in her mid-twenties with purple dreadlocks and several facial piercings unlocked the bar. Horace and Carol barreled in and flopped down on two of the five stools at the tiny bar. A man with clothing too tight, a flap of black hair, an overgrown beard, and thick black frame glasses waited on them. Carol and Horace ordered more beer. I took a seat at the bar and asked for water. Horace and Carol ridiculed me for not drinking. The bartender nodded at my request and understood I was a designated driver, giving me a sympathetic smile. Here was a man who knew what it was like to be the only sober person in a room full of slobbering drunks. Being the only one sober wasn't fun, especially when all you wanted was to be left alone, or in the case of the bartender, to do your job. Actually, dealing with the two drunken dickheads was downright annoying. My head was going to explode eventually if I kept biting my tongue whenever they did something that bothered me.

After a couple of drinks Carol began to flirt with the bartender which notably made him extremely uncomfortable. Horace began his usual tactic of berating the guy with nonstop questions about his personal life and constantly placing a cigarette between his lips and having to be told he couldn't smoke in the bar. As slyly as I could I convinced the two we should get something to eat and we moved to the restaurant section down a narrow hallway at the back of the building. The entrance to the restaurant section had a low ceiling. Horace managed to smack his forehead on the doorjamb.

"Ow! God damn it!" Horace yelped.

I said, "I told you to watch your head. This building is old."

Horace rubbed his forehead. He already had a slightly purpled mark on the skin when he removed his hand. A part of me gloated in the discomfort he would feel when he woke up tomorrow. Carol laughed.

Horace bellowed, "Shut up, whore!"

"Keep it down," I said. "I want to get something to eat before we get kicked out."

We were the only patrons in the place. I sat at a booth and the other two sat across from me. The two took in their surroundings. The room was claustrophobic and constructed of old timber held together by ancient nails and some type of mortar. There was a plaque on the wall explaining the building was constructed in 1847 and was the oldest standing building in the town.

Carol said, "I've lived around here for a while and I've never been in this place." She spotted the jukebox hidden in the shadows. "Oh! Oh!" She smacked Horace's arm. "Give me a dollar."

"I'm not giving you shit!" he said.

"You're an asshole," she said. "I don't have any cash. Please."

Her hand disappeared under the table and she began to rub what I assumed was his thigh. She laid her head on his shoulder and begged him again. He lifted her hand and threw it back in her direction.

"Get off my dick! Make your own money, you stupid slut. If people are really into your fat naked photos why aren't they paying for them?"

Carol stared at him with a stupefied expression. It was evident she'd never considered the possibility she could make a profit from her exhibition.

She recovered from her dumbfounded state and laughed in a derisive manner. "I'm an artist, Horace. I don't care if I make money from my photos. I want to display a woman's body in all of its glory. My photos are an art form." She took another drink of her beer and became more interested in staring at the jukebox.

"Call it what you want," Horace said. "You're taking off your clothes. Some sad fuck is jerking of to your pathetic photos. And you're constantly broke. It seems like you might be retarded."

I interjected, "Mentally challenged."

"What?!" Horace barked.

I repeated, "Mentally cha—"

"Oh, Jesus Christ! I don't give a fuck!"

The waitress appeared with menus. It was the girl who opened the bar for us. She placed three menus on the table and gave us an uneasy smile. It was apparent she thought the three of us were going to be a problem. Anyone would the way Horace continually shouted while intoxicated. I tried to give her an apologetic smile when I saw the wheels turning in Horace's head. He scrutinized her with an angry expression.

The waitress said, "Hello. My name's Liberty and I'll be your server." She retrieved a notepad from the back pocket of her tight jeans. "Can I start you guys off with something to drink?" She pulled a pen hidden somewhere within her ratted hair and positioned it above the pad.

"Beer," Horace said. "A pitcher."

"What kind? We have dom—"

"I don't care." He waved at her dismissively. "Whatever's the strongest."

The waitress didn't scribble anything on the pad. She redirected her gaze to Carol who had pushed her breasts together in a seductive manner while Horace barked his order.

Carol lifted her beer and spoke in a soft and flirtatious tone. "I'll share his. Do you guys have any dollars for the jukebox?"

Liberty pointed her pen back toward the bar. "There's an ATM by the door."

Carol spoke in a baby voice. "I can't get a dollar from you?"

Liberty's smile became more uneasy. "Sorry."

Carol pouted, leaned back, and crossed her arms over her breasts. Liberty looked to me.

"Can I get a cola?"

The waitress nodded and disappeared.

Horace flipped through the menu and said, "I don't know why you flirt with women. You're not gay."

I opened my menu but already knew what I wanted.

"Guys think it's hot for two girls to fuck." Carol addressed me. "Don't you think it's hot when two women lick each other's slits?"

"Me?" I said.

"Yeah," she said. "All men think two girls having sex is hot. I pretend I'm into girls all the time to get attention from men."

"Honestly," I said. "I think it's sort of sick."

"Because you're a prude," she sneered. "And a homophobe."

Anger pulsed through my chest and I clenched my jaw. "Not two women having sex. The fact you *fake* being gay to get attention. I think it's sick and you're fucking demented to take on such a plight. Don't you think homosexuals have enough struggles without people accusing them of pretending so they get attention because someone else did? It's gotta be hell when people tell them it's a phase because some girl thought it would be cute to make out with a couple of her friends while she was in college while *they're* genuinely struggling with their sexuality."

Carol stared at me open-mouthed.

Horace laughed. "There's the testy Abe I know. Where have you been?"

"Annoyed by having to corral two drunks."

Carol said, "I'm not hurting gay people when I make out with a woman."

"When was the last time you kissed a woman?" Horace said and responded for her. "Never! Because even women think you're gross!"

"I'm not a prude," I said. "I've had plenty of satisfying sex in my lifetime. My wife and I fucked frequently until the day she died. We did a lot of things that may be considered illegal in some states. I personally think your idea of sex is fucking warped and disgusting. And you're disgusting. You try to use your sexuality to gain things and you think it's a weapon you can use to manipulate people. It's a form of prostitution, that's what it is. And I think you're crass and gauche and you're physically, intellectually, and emotionally repugnant."

Horace roared with laughter and slapped the table.

My gaze snapped to him. "Shut up. Or I'll lay into you next and make you cry like a big baby with too much money."

The waitress returned with our drinks. She said, "Have you had time to look at the menu? Do you know what you want?" She produced her pen and pad again.

"Can I get a burger," I said. "Medium rare with fries."

Horace said, "Rare isn't good for you." He proceeded to fill his glass from the pitcher of beer.

"I don't care," I said. "I'm pretty sure drinking isn't good for you either."

Liberty jotted down my order and looked at Carol.

Carol recovered from my critique and continued to flirt with Liberty. She tried to mimic Marilyn Monroe and said, "Fried pickles and tater tots."

Horace said, "You eat like a child."

"And for you," Liberty said addressing Horace.

"I'll have the grilled chicken with a side salad. Vinaigrette dressing," he said.

We all folded our menus and handed them to her. She turned to retreat to the kitchen to place our orders but was stopped by Horace.

"Tell me something, Liberty," Horace said. He made a steeple with his fingers, placed them in front of his lips, and furrowed his brows. "Why did ya fuck with your face like that?"

"Horace," I reprimanded him.

He turned to me with an angry expression. "What?! I'm curious why an intelligent human being would want to look like they fell into a tackle box. It's dumb. She looks stupid!"

"You're an asshole," Carol said. "I think she's hot."

"You'd think a rotting corpse was fuckable!" Horace shouted.

Liberty appeared stricken and said, "I'm sorry you feel that way."

I leaned close to Liberty and said, "Don't apologize to him. He's invasive and rude and doesn't know how to act in social situations."

Horace rolled his hand in the air for her to continue. "Please enlighten us with your intellectual reasons for fucking up your face and hair."

"Don't answer him," I said. "You can't win. He only wants to degrade you to make himself feel better. It's what he does."

Horace glared at me and opened his mouth to retort but nothing came.

The waitress produced a dollar from her pocket and slammed it down on the table beside Carol. "A gift for the jukebox so none of us have to listen to this pompous ass." She leaned her head toward Horace.

Liberty turned abruptly and disappeared down the hall toward the bar. Carol snatched up the money and did a giddy little dance in her seat like a child before jumping up and making her way to the jukebox.

Horace strained his neck and shouted toward the hall Liberty fled down. "I wouldn't fuck her anyway! I bet her pubic hair is all matted and smelly like the hair on her head!" He leaned toward me. "She's not getting a tip."

"Do you always have to get the last word in?" I said. "You *better* tip the poor girl. God knows she deserves one for putting up with your shit."

He smiled. "I'm joking! I would still fuck her. I bet she has a massive bush. I like girls who have a lot of hair on their puss. Girls shave it all off now. Guys too. Have you seen porn lately?"

"I'm depressed. Not dead. I've seen po—"

"Nobody has any hair! It's like a bunch of grown naked babies having sex! It's sick!"

"You're sick."

The jukebox blared a god awful compilation of computer noises and a whiney female voice. Carol was facing the contraption and made a whopping noise. She threw her arms in the air and slowly lowered them. She stroked her face and body. She swung her hips back and forth in a rhythm that didn't match the beat of the music. After a few seconds she spun around to face us and lip sync to the lyrics. She made her way to us while dancing in a jerky fashion resembling some type of zombie stagger or a fit of seizures. I'm sure she'd practiced the maneuvers several times in front of a mirror and thought it made her sensual but her off beat movements combined with her unappetizing appearance made her look sad and desperate. The volume of the music made it impossible for Horace and I to continue our conversation and since we were the only people in the room we were forced to give Carol our undivided attention. Once she made it to us she grabbed the edge of our table and began to thrash her head around, making her hair a part of the performance. Horace watched her with an annoyed expression and I became concerned she might hurt herself. She released her grip on the table top and took a step back. She turned around and bent over to give us a view of her enormous and cellulite riddled behind. Her skirt rode up and we were subjected to a view of her hairy vagina as she tried desperately to bounce her rear end. Her body was years past the vibrancy it needed to perform the act correctly. Instead the action reminded me of dimpled Jell-O or cottage cheese in an earthquake. As the song came to an end she stood and stumbled before taking her seat next to Horace. My ears rang in the new found silence.

Horace said, "That was pathetic."

Carol chugged her beer. She was covered in sweat. She set the beer down and panted, "Whatevs."

"You know you're not thirteen," Horace said.

"I don't think thirteen-year-olds dance that way," I said.

Horace laughed. "Are you kidding me? You don't watch much TV, do you? Thirteen-year-olds dress and act like twenty-year-old strippers! They're fucking middle-aged men and they wear clothes that don't cover anything. They barely have tits and pubic hair! We live in a world overrun with Lolitas."

"That's my favorite book," Carol said.

Horace guffawed. "It's probably the only book you've ever read."

Carol ignored him. "I can't believe you only get one song for a dollar. Do either of you have a dollar?"

I had cash in my wallet but I didn't want to be subjected to another sad display of Carol trying to be seductive. She was suffering from a bad case of being way past her prime and overcompensated by trying to be youthful by today's standards. I remembered when Beverly went through the same phase in her fifties. She had a meltdown full of 'I'm not as pretty as I used to be' and 'How can you still find me attractive when I look like an old hag'. She and our daughter went on a full makeover and shopping spree at my expense. They bought all new clothes and spent a couple hundred dollars at a salon. When Beverly came home her long salt and pepper hair had been replaced with a bleached bob and her clothes were something a twenty-year-old would wear. She was happy for a couple of weeks even though I thought it was ridiculous. I never told her I thought she had lost her mind though. That's what men *do*. We tell the women in our lives they are beautiful no matter what because every woman, even if she doesn't admit it, is insecure and wants to be found attractive not only by the man in her life but by every male they encounter. But after a few weeks her hair began to grow out and all the years of hardship she was trying to hide with hair dye were right there. Those roots screamed 'See . . . under all this I'm still an old woman' and it sent her into another fit. But this time she was overwrought with the realization that hair color and clothes ultimately could not turn back the hands of time. New clothes could not erase the wrinkles from her face or give her the vitality she once had.

Carol made bedroom eyes at me, waiting for an answer. I shook my head.

She held her hand out in front of Horace's face. "Give me a dollar."

"Quit asking me for money," Horace snapped. "You're socially barbarous. Isn't it enough you're mooching my beer?" He took another drink, which ended up being half of the glass's contents.

Carol began to whine like a child but was cut off when Liberty materialized with our food. She set down our plates, dropped a ketchup and mustard bottle in the middle of the table, and asked if we needed anything else. Liberty barely waited a beat, none of us answering her, before she left.

Carol and I began to eat in silence and Horace glanced at our plates with a disapproving sneer before digging in. Carol moaned while she ate as if the bar food was the best meal she'd ever consumed.

After a few minutes Horace picked up the pitcher of beer to refill his empty glass. He scrutinized the small amount left. "We need more beer."

I was fed up with the two and their drunken behavior.

More alcohol consumption was not going to make the situation better.

I masticated my food and swallowed. "Why don't we go back to my place when we're done?" Having them in my home wasn't ideal either but the only other option was to abandon them.

"No," Carol whined around a mouthful of food.

Horace said, "Going to your house doesn't fix the fact I don't have anything to drink with my dinner."

I pushed my glass of cola toward him. "Share mine." I regretted it once I'd said it, not knowing exactly where Horace's mouth had been. I glanced at Carol and repressed a shudder.

Horace said, "Do you know how many empty calories are in soda?"

"Then die of thirst," I said. "I was trying to be nice." I pulled the glass toward me.

More than anything I was trying to keep Horace's interactions with the waitress to a minimum. I couldn't conclude anything good would come of it. I wasn't a frequent visitor to any of the eating establishments in town but, nonetheless, it was a small town and I didn't want to be remembered as the guy who came in here one time with two slobbering assholes and started a ruckus.

Horace lifted Carol's beer and downed it.

"Hey!" Carol protested.

He set the empty glass on the table. "It was my beer anyway."

I had a brief flashback to when the kids were small, fighting in the backseat of the car while I drove. Now Horace and Carol began to bicker. I tuned them out to finish my meal. I finished my burger and fries while the other two were barely halfway through their meals. I was done. Not only done with my food but with them. I couldn't stand to be around them anymore. I never could tolerate procrastinators. I thought of the kids again. About how'd they used to piss around getting their coats and shoes on to go to an appointment or a store. And I'd stand there with my car keys in hand, ready to go ten minutes previous, while they fucked around. Eventually I refused to take them anywhere and made Beverly stay at home with them until they grew to be teenagers and able to take care of themselves. But when they were young they always managed to turn a simple ten minute trip to the store into an hour and a half debacle of dawdling and whining and begging until I felt as if my head would explode from trying to suppress my anger and frustration in public.

I stood.

Horace's attention snapped to me, mid-argument. "Where are you going?"

"Home."

"But we're still eating!"

I shrugged. "You know where I live. I need some air."

"Come on!"

I slammed my fist down on the table. "Enough!" The silverware on our plates jumped. The outburst startled the two. It startled me. I was never one to exhibit anger outside of my home but I wasn't going to back down. "I'm not in the mood to sit around and watch you two fucking argue all day. I told you I wasn't in the mood for drinking an—"

"Lighten up," Horace said.

"Stop interrupting me! And quit trying to placate me!"

"I'm not," Horace said and laughed.

Carol giggled like a brainless idiot. I clenched my jaw. I was overwhelmed with the compulsion to punch Horace in the face and knew I needed to get away from them. I turned and fled before my anger surged into new territory. Horace hollered for me to come back. I ran into Liberty halfway down the hall. I produced my wallet, handed her two twenties, and mumbled for her to keep the change for her trouble. I knew Horace would stiff her out of a tip.

I exited the bar and the bright sunlight stabbed my eyes. I squinted and shielded my eyes from the sun's rays. I waited a few seconds for my eyes to adjust before I proceeded to make my way home. As I walked, I entertained the thought of swallowing all the pills when I arrived home. End it all now. But I knew I wouldn't or couldn't let this be my last day or the final moments of my life. I didn't want to die angry. I wanted to go out on my own terms. I planned it. I would die with the loving thoughts of Beverly and it would be calm and relaxing, not in a rush of spitefulness and exhausted anger from dealing with two drunks. I didn't know what Horace and Carol planned for the rest of the day and I didn't care. I was going to have another quiet evening alone. The same as I'd done the day before. I would try again tomorrow. I was overwrought with dread once I was within eyeshot of my house, knowing my plans were once again shat on by Horace's presence. His car sat in my driveway. I was so involved with my own thoughts and plans I'd forgotten that he'd driven to my house. The two of them would be back eventually. And the best I could hope for at this point was for them to leave shortly after.

5

My evening was quiet. The phone didn't ring often anymore but it was a relief not to even think about it. I should have destroyed the damn thing years ago.

When I first became one of Dr. Wiwi's sales reps I thought it would be an easy way to supplement my measly retirement from my data entry job. I'd never been much of an advocate for a nine to five job. The vapid people I worked with sucked my will to live with their endless conversations about the food they'd consumed or were going to consume that night and whatever television programs were popular at the moment. I couldn't take some dawdling idiot holding a cup of coffee, staring out a window and off into the middle distance, and giving a real time weather report by announcing it was raining or sunny outside. If I had to endure one more day of an office full of brainwashed parrots who talked about insipid garbage just to be talking I thought I was going to lose it. I decided the best thing for me was to retire early at the age of fifty. I wanted to enjoy the last years of my life as much as possible and not work my fingers to the bone. With the early retirement came a huge cut in my benefits. Beverly and I were all right but it didn't leave us much wiggle room. She complained she wanted to go on vacations. She said she wanted to go to the Grand Canyon and throw trash in it, something she'd said everyone was doing and she'd seen on a television program. She threatened to find a job of her own. She'd never worked a day in her life and it killed me to see her searching the want ads. Then one day I found an ad in the back of one of Beverly's magazines. It boasted 'work from home' and 'easy money' and 'all you need is an Internet connection and a phone'. I thought it would be a clever way for us to have more financial freedom while I could stay at home every day and not have to deal with the mindless drones in an office setting. All I had to do was call the phone numbers on the list provided from the company and read a script. The goal was to convince people they needed the subliminal self-help cassettes. The script guaranteed they would lose weight or quit smoking or gain confidence or fix whatever shortcoming, insecurity, or self-loathing attribute they wanted to change. There were a hundred different tapes and a billion more fuck off responses when people answered their phones. And the people who *were* interested wanted the CD version, to which there was none. For some reason Dr. Wiwi was never compelled to update his product. And then the 'do not call' list was instated in 2003 and I went from making cold calls to waiting for the phone to ring. Dr. Wiwi switched out his help wanted ad to an advertisement explaining all the benefits of his tapes along with a phone number for ordering. My phone number. I tried several times to contact the company to fix the problem but gave up after being given the run around and put on hold a thousand times. What did it matter though? Hardly any calls actually came in and I still got paid.

I wandered the house listlessly. I didn't bother turning on the TV or the radio. The silence was occasionally broken by a neighbor's dog or a passing motorcycle. I avoided spending too much time looking at photos of Beverly and the kids hanging on the walls.

The quiet finally came to an end around nine in the evening. I heard the two idiots carrying on as they walked down the road. I checked out the kitchen window. Carol and Horace leaned on one another as they approached the house. The nosey old woman across the street was also peering out one of her windows, watching the two with a disapproving scowl on her face. A wave of embarrassment washed over me when the two started up my drive. Horace noticed me in the window. He waved and laughed at me. The embarrassment of the neighbor noticing the two crass morons were my company quickly wore off. Panic replaced the embarrassment once they passed Horace's car and headed for my door.

How could I be so stupid? I should've known they wouldn't leave. Why didn't I lock the doors and shut the lights off before they got back? I could've pretended I was asleep or wasn't home.

Carol stumbled and almost fell. Horace caught her but nearly fell also. I stopped beating myself up and knew I couldn't let the two lushes drive anywhere. I was baffled the two of them were conscious and alive after the amount of alcohol they'd ingested.

I met them at the door. The two practically fell into my house. They laughed and stumbled around, clutching one another, and I wasn't sure if Carol was helping Horace stay upright or the other way around.

Horace laid his hand on the dining table for support, his arm around Carol's neck. There was a light purple mark under his eye, adding to the faint bruise on his forehead from hitting his head in the bar. I assessed the rest of him. His clothes were disheveled and there were grass stains on his jeans.

I said, "Have you been fighting?"

Carol burst into a bray of laughter and snorted.

Horace's speech was severely slurred, "Fuck that guy! He wouldn't stop staring at me like a homo! Fucking . . . Fucking rednecks! Go fuck a sheep!"

Carol laughed and crumbled to the floor. She rolled around laughing while her short skirt rode up with every movement until her ass and genitalia were exposed. Horace staggered without her support and collapsed unceremoniously onto one of the dining room chairs, nearly toppling it.

I sighed. "Jesus, Horace."

"Can we crash here tonight?" he said.

"Are the police going to show up? How much trouble are you in?"

Carol made it into a sitting position but made no attempt to adjust her skirt and cover herself. Her face was pointed in my direction but her eyes were closed. She sported a shit-eating grin. "They told us they wouldn't call the cops if we left," she said in a childlike voice.

Horace stood and staggered. "I'm going to bed." He stumbled into the kitchen.

Carol made it to her hands and knees and crawled after him, her ass still exposed. I told them to take the bedroom at the end of the hall but Horace made a beeline toward the bathroom across the hallway from my room. He left the door open and I was forced to follow Carol as she continued to crawl. She found her way into my bedroom. I yelled at her to keep going down the hall but she ignored me. Horace began retching in the bathroom and I turned my attention to him. He was on his knees leaning over the bathtub with his hands on the ledge. A fountain of beer and whatever food was in his stomach expelled into the tub and splattered on the shower walls.

"Oh god damn it! Use the toilet!" I said.

He managed to tell me he wasn't feeling good before he released another torrent. Carol began laughing and I left Horace. My room was dark and I flipped the light switch. Carol was completely naked and rolling around on my bed.

Calmly, I said, "Get the fuck out of my bed."

Carol said, "It's okay. You can sleep with us too. I'll take both of you at the same time." She played with one of her saggy breasts and began to masturbate. "I'll let you fuck me in the ass."

I roared, "Get the fuck out!" and charged toward her.

She tried to roll away from me. I grabbed her wrist and yanked her. She yelped. She weighed more than I expected and I barely managed to budge her.

Horace stumbled into the room. "Are you fucking my girlfriend?"

Carol cried, "Rape!"

I threw her arm back at her and managed to smack her in the face with her own hand. She began to cry.

"I'll kick your ass!" Horace yelled. He tried to tackle me but ended up on the floor.

"I don't want anything to do with your whore!" I shouted. "I want both of you out of my room! This is my room! This is my marital bed! I want you to get the fuck out!" I pointed to the door. I could feel my pulse in my temples.

Horace grabbed the edge of the mattress and got to his feet. "Come on, Carol."

He took her hand as she sobbed softly. I didn't feel sorry for slapping her with her own hand. There are some boundaries you don't cross and masturbating in my wife's bed was one of them. Horace helped her out of bed and into the correct bedroom. I shut the door behind them. I could hear Horace trying to soothe her and after a minute her sobs subsided.

Carol's clothes were scattered on the floor of my room. I opened my door and kicked them out into the hallway and in front of their door. I wasn't about to touch them. God knew what kind of STDs she had.

I was exhausted but knew I'd better clean up the vomit in the tub before turning in. I held my breath before entering the bathroom and pulled the collar of my shirt over my nose. The tub was a disaster. I pulled the curtain half closed and turned the shower on. Chunks of food stopped the drain. I found the rubber cleaning gloves under the vanity, scooped up the food, and dumped it in the toilet. I gagged until my eyes watered. Once the tub was clean I sprayed it with some bleach cleaner and flushed the toilet before deciding to clean it too.

When I was finished I scrubbed my hands, checked the doors of the house to make sure they were locked, and turned off the lights with the exception of the bathroom in case either of the idiots needed to use it in the middle of the night. I threw the comforter on the floor, since Carol had fouled it, and collapsed into bed. It was the earliest I'd gone to bed in a long time and the deepest I'd slept since Beverly's death.

6

"A be. Abe."

Someone jostled my shoulder. I opened my eyes. Horace was leaning over me in his underwear.

"How do you make the shower work? There's no damn knob on the faucet."

"Um." I tried to clear the fog of sleep from my brain. "The faucet itself."

"What?"

"The faucet is the knob. Where the water comes out. Grab the round piece and pull down." I threw the covers off and started to sit up. "I'll show you."

"No no. You get some sleep." He took some steps backward toward the door.

"Are you sure?"

"Yeah. I'll figure it out." He exited my room and shut the door.

I flopped back down in bed and checked the alarm

clock. It was a few minutes past eight o'clock in the morning. I managed to sleep close to nine hours. I couldn't remember the last time I'd slept more than four hours. It was before Beverly's death. Sleep didn't come easy once she was gone. And what hours I did manage to get each night were filled with horrible night terrors. I usually woke myself screaming or bawling like a child. But the nine hours of sleep must not have been enough and I slipped off into a dreamless slumber again.

The second time Horace woke me he wasn't as polite.

"Get up."

Horace was dressed. He stared down at me with a scowl on his face and held a rolled up piece of paper.

I asked, "What time is it?" while simultaneously searching for the clock.

Horace smacked me in the face with the paper like an owner correcting a dog for shitting on the floor. It didn't hurt much but it was unexpected and pissed me off to be fucked with upon waking.

"Hey!" I yelled. "What the hell did you do that for, ya idiot?"

He hit me again.

I threw the blanket off. "God damn it! Quit fucking with me!"

I got to my feet and lunged at him. I tried to grab the paper from him so he would stop hitting me with it. The grogginess of sleep left me stiff and slow and he yanked his arm back before I could grab the paper. He held it above his head in a taunting manner and extended his other arm to keep me away. I gave up the squabble after a few seconds. I didn't give a shit about the paper. I didn't want to get hit in the face anymore.

Horace frowned when he unrolled the paper and began to read. "Dear Nathan and Tara. I'm sorry. I can't live without your mother. She was all I've known for the last fourty-five years. I can't live with the ghost of her memory. I thought it would get better with time but it has only gotten worse. Just know I'm happier with her. Dad."

His fiery stare bored through me. Embarrassment flushed my face for a brief moment and anger suddenly replaced my chagrin.

I said, "You snooped through my stuff."

"You spelled forty wrong."

I snatched the paper from him and wadded it up. "You're an invasive asshole! I gave you a place to sleep and you repay me by snooping! I think you and your girl-friend have overstayed your welcome and it's time to go."

"I wasn't snooping! It was lying on your desk and I wanted to use your computer!"

I threw the balled up paper at him. It hit him in the chest and bounced to the floor. I grabbed his arm to escort him out but he jerked away from me.

"I'm not going anywhere," he said. "Abe . . . you're go-ing to kill yourself?"

I couldn't discern whether his tone was concern or con-fusion. Either way his discovery of the letter was humiliat-ing and the shame infuriated me.

"So what if I am?" I said. "It's none of your business. It's no one's business." I pointed at him. "You didn't give two shits about me before you read that fucking letter. I told you I was depressed and you laughed it off. You thought it was a joke. My kids haven't visited since the funeral because they have their own lives and can't be bothered with me. And I'm here all alone with her memory and the memory of the face she made right before she died! I can't stop thinking about it!"

"Come on," he said. "Your kids give a fuck."

I laughed. "No, they don't. They're assholes. Don't believe me? I'll show you."

I stormed out of the bedroom. Behind the guest bedroom door Carol was trying to sing some song I didn't recognize and failing. Once in my office I headed straight for the answering machine and hit the play button. Horace stood in the doorway. I skipped a couple of saved messages until the one from last Saturday began. I watched Horace's face for his reaction.

Nathan's voice was bored and disinterested. "Hey, Dad. It's Nathan. Was just making the weekly call." Long pause. Nathan sighed. "Guess I'll call next Saturday." The message stopped and began to play the next message. I stopped the machine.

Horace crossed his arms over his chest, furrowed his brow, and nodded. In a mocking tone he said, "You're right. Sounds like a huge asshole."

I shouted, "He's not calling me because he gives a fuck! He's calling because he feels obligated!"

"And that's why you were going to kill yourself?"

"You wouldn't understand." I rubbed my eyes partly to clear away the sleep but mainly from frustration. "Your wife left you. She didn't die. You guys hated each other."

"I didn't hate my wife. She lost interest in me and wanted to move on."

"Your wife quit sleeping with you because you couldn't keep your dick out of other people and you're an insufferable human being."

He opened his mouth to retort but the guest bedroom

door opened. Carol barged into the office. She'd slept in her makeup and her black eyeliner and mascara were streaked under her eyes. She wore an enormous white ball gown, slightly yellowed from age. It was several sizes too small and her chubby old lady arms, breasts, and waist threatened to bust all the seams. She was unable to fasten the back. She grinned like a moron and sashayed her hips back and forth to fan the ballooned floor length skirt. I wondered where she'd obtained the dress since she didn't bring a bag. Then I suddenly recognized the garment.

"Isn't it pretty?" Carol said. She held her phone at arm's length above her head, struck an openmouthed porn pose, and snapped a photo before furiously typing away on her screen.

I said, "I am going to murder you if you don't take that off right fucking now."

Her smile disappeared. "But it was hanging in the closet—"

I screamed something indecipherable and charged her. She squealed and tried to hide behind Horace. I ran into both of them and all three of us tumbled into the hallway. I fell on top of Horace and he yelped in pain. Carol smacked the back of her head into the wall and left a dent in the drywall. She clutched her head and began to cry. Horace tried to shove me off but I was determined to get to Carol. I grabbed at her arm but she jerked away. She continued to cry and refocused her attention on smacking me in the head. I tried to shield her blows with one arm.

Blindly, I groped for the dress and took up a handful of it. "Take it off!" I bellowed.

Carol wrenched away and the excruciating sound of Beverly's wedding dress tearing brought all the commotion to a complete stop. I froze holding the dress in one hand with my other arm covering my head to keep Carol from giving me brain damage. I uncovered my head and looked to Horace, who's eyes were enormous in shock and expectation, then I turned my attention to Carol's frightened face, and finally I focused on the enormous rip between the torso and the skirt of my dead wife's wedding dress. I let go of the skirt and my face contorted, in miniscule increments and ticks, to a mask of pure rage.

Horace gently pushed me off him. I rolled onto my back and stared at the ceiling, wishing the whole house would spontaneously combust. Horace got to his knees and put himself between me and Carol.

Horace leaned over me so all I could see was his dumb face. "Abe?"

I couldn't respond. I could if I wanted to but I was afraid of myself. Not once in my entire life was I as angry as I was at that moment. I was afraid to open my mouth because I didn't know what would come out. A howl of rage? Expletives? An oath to murder Carol? Or maybe I would break down and bawl. None of the options were appealing so I shut down.

Horace repeated my name. I shook my head at him, trying to convey my reluctance to speak. He turned and told Carol to go back into the bedroom and change. Her retreat was accompanied by the rustle of the dress and punctuated by the click of the bedroom door shutting. Once she was clear of the hallway Horace put his hands under my shoulders and forced me to sit up.

"Come on," he said. "Let's get some breakfast. Then we can go get something to drink."

There was no point in repeating for the hundredth time

I wasn't in the mood to drink. I wasn't even in the mood for food. I wanted both of them to leave. *I* was ready to leave. The world was filled with inconsiderate people with their own self-fulfilling agenda and none of them could see how, little by little, their actions killed the will of people similar to me in small doses every day until we were dead inside and dead to the world and were ready to check out. I resigned and allowed him to help me up and to the kitchen. I would be an agreeable zombie for now. If all else failed I could lead both of them out of the house with a ploy of more alcohol and tell them I forgot something and double back, lock them out, and call the police if they didn't get in their car and leave. I was trapped inside a warped home invasion nightmare.

Horace followed me to the kitchen. I busied myself with preparing breakfast while he leaned against the counter. He did most of the talking. I defrosted a pound of bacon and cooked the whole package, scrambled all of the remaining eggs, which amounted to three quarters of a carton, and toasted six pieces of bread. Either Horace did not notice the massive amount of food I was preparing, didn't care, or he was under the same assumption I was— Carol was a big girl and would complain if she couldn't stuff her face until her stomach was on the verge of exploding. I prepared a pot of coffee and set the food out in an assembly line fashion on the counter along with salt, pepper, butter, ketchup and tabasco. Horace and I prepared a rational amount of food for ourselves and proceeded to the dining room. Horace announced loudly to Carol there was food in the kitchen.

Horace sat across from me and began to eat quickly. He spoke around a mouthful of food. "You've been quiet.

Are you in a better mood? Less suicidal?"

Somewhere in the house Carol sang and I thought she sounded the way a live cat in a blender would sound. A couple of doors opened and closed. I could make out the sound of the bathroom faucet. I suppressed the urge to grab my hair and rip handfuls of it out. The sheer presence of her drove me up the walls.

"I'm tired," I said. I sipped my coffee. "I'm tired of no one else in the world seeing almost everything they do is wrong, pigheaded, and idiotic. And I'm sick of those people getting butt hurt when someone finally stands up and tells them they're an asshole. They're so deluded and medicated and they've been given gold stars *just* for participating. They can't wrap their heads around the idea they might be wrong and not everyone in the world agrees with them. And people don't have to like them and they are not the hot shit they think they are. I'm tired of people having self-made and inflated self-confidence because of social networking. They're fuckups and losers like the rest of us." I picked up my fork and took a bite of my scrambled eggs.

"You *are* in a good mood!" He laughed.

I swallowed my food. "Let me be blunt—"

"Were you being circuitous?"

"Some people must think so. I'm telling you . . . I hate ninety-five percent of the people I meet and I'm only able to tolerate four percent of the ones I don't hate in about twenty minute intervals. I hate your girlfriend and she's stayed *way* past her welcome. She's a fucking asshole and you're lucky I didn't cunt punt her into next year for defiling Beverly's wedding dress."

He furrowed his brows. "Come on, man—"

I pointed my fork at him. "If you defend her you're a

bigger asshole than she is." I stabbed another lump of egg. "Besides, you don't like her either."

His expression relaxed and he shrugged. "Touché."

We continued our breakfast in silence. Through the doorway I spotted Carol in the kitchen. She began to load a plate with *all* of the remaining food. I wondered why she even bothered with a plate. She could've grazed at the counter and saved me a dish to clean. I turned my attention to the mail on the table I neglected the previous day. I tossed the electric bill aside and a few circulars that were irrelevant to me because they were for Beverly. The final piece of post was from Dr. Wiwi's office. It wasn't the standard envelope I received my checks in. The envelope was larger and the contents thicker. I opened it and found a formal looking invitation, similar to a wedding announcement, inviting me to an awards ceremony for the top sellers of Dr. Wiwi's subliminal self-help tapes. The award ceremony was two days away and was to be held in the lobby of a Holiday Inn Express in Covington, Virginia. I'd never heard of Covington and there was probably a reason I hadn't. Who has events in the lobby of a hotel? Weren't those types of ceremonies held in banquet halls? Why was I now getting an invitation with only two days till the event? People normally planned well in advance and the guests should've been given ample time to arrange their trip.

Carol entered the dining room and sat beside Horace. She began to eat as though she hadn't eaten in a week. She'd removed her makeup and her appearance drew my attention away from the invitation. There was something desperate about her sad body mixed with the youthful attire and makeup I found repulsive the day before. But without the makeup she appeared ghoulish. Her face was heavily wrinkled and age spotted. The large dark circles under her eyes made them appear sunken. She definitely needed some help from Mary Kay because whatever her current cosmetic regimen was it needed a serious update. She was unaware I was staring at her and I returned my attention to the invitation.

I read the card again, shook my head, gave a small derisive laugh, and tossed it on the table. I picked up my fork and continued my breakfast.

Carol looked at the card and recognized it as something important. "Oh," she said and picked up the invitation. "What's this?" Her eyes scanned the writing. "A wedding invitation?"

"No!" I said. I reached across the table and snatched it from her. "It's my mail and a federal offense to pilfer it." I threw the card down and it landed in front of Horace, print side up.

Carol gave me a wounded look. "What does pilfer mean?"

Horace tilted his head to read the card. "It means to steal, idiot."

"I'm not an idiot!" She turned to me. "And I wasn't stealing. I was reading it."

"So you could crash a wedding," Horace said. He looked up from the card. "'Dr. Wiwi cordially invites you—'" He interrupted himself with laughter and repeated the name Wiwi.

I snatched up the invitation, this time ripped it in half, and threw it on the floor before returning to my food.

"Hey! What did ya do that for?" Horace said.

I said, "Stay out of my business."

"Are ya gonna go?"

"No."

"Why not?"

I set my fork down and counted on my fingers. "Because it's unnecessary. I don't have the money. The ceremony is two days away. And it smells fishy . . . it's probably a hoax." I took a sip of coffee.

"But don't you want to meet the doctor?"

There was a part of me that did want to meet the guy. I wanted to know why he'd never updated to CDs and how my phone number became the number to phone in orders. How could there be a sales ceremony if I was the only person receiving the sales? I imagined Dr. Wiwi's disembodied voice was the one narrating the tapes. He sounded British and older and the image I conjured was one of an old man sitting around reading dusty hardcover books in a smoking jacket by a fireplace and he smoked a pipe while reading with a self-satisfied smirk on his lips because he'd found a way to make money while other people did all the work for him.

I said, "Not really."

"Yes you do," Horace said. "Hell, I want to meet him. I want to know who the guy is."

Carol finished the last of her food. "Can I come?"

"We're not going anywhere," I said.

She slumped in her chair, crossed her arms, and pouted like a child.

"Come on!" Horace yelled. "What else do you have to do? Sit around here and think about killing yourself?"

"Yes."

He leaned toward the floor and retrieved the two pieces of the invitation. He held them together, placed them on the table, and read the information again. "You could drive to this. Virginia isn't far."

I said, "Do you have any idea how large the state of Ohio is? Virginia isn't a small state either. God knows where Covington is."

Carol produced her phone from between her breasts and typed on the screen furiously. "From Yellow Springs it's less than five hours."

Horace said, "See? Five hours is a day trip."

Carol stared at her plate, forlorn. "Do you have any more bacon?"

"I made *all* the bacon," I said.

"I'm still hungry," she whined. She extended her phone holding arm at a strange angle and took a photo of herself and another photo of her empty plate.

"I think you should go," Horace said. "We can take my car. I'll pay for gas and the hotel."

Carol clapped and squealed. "Road trip!" She began to type on her phone and contorted her lips to form the words she was typing.

I said, "I honestly don't think I can stand to be around you people anymore."

"Don't be a wuss," Horace said.

"I'm not a wuss. I don't want to go. It's pointless. What am I going to gain from wasting my time on some pathetic ceremony—"

"The experience. You really need to get out of this house for a couple of days. Go out and see the world for fuck's sake! Maybe you wouldn't be so goddamn depressed if you tried to have some fun every once in a while."

"I doubt it."

"Well, then, we're not leaving until you go."

"Don't be asinine."

"I'm serious. I'm not leaving." He crossed his arms over his chest.

"I guess I'll have to call the cops and tell them about the two pathetic trespassers in my house. I'll let them know how you got that black eye."

Carol said, "I don't think we're trespassing if you invited us in."

I said, "I should've checked for your reflection before I let *you* in."

"What does *that* mean?" she said.

Horace said, "Are you gonna call the cops on the phone in the garbage? I noticed that too when I was in your office. I guess you'll have to use your cell phone. Oh, wait a minute, you don't have one."

"Ohhhhhh, snap!" Carol said.

"Shut up," I barked at her.

Carol giggled and Horace stared at me with a smug smile. He raised his eyebrows as if asking me what my next move would be.

7

They didn't leave. They commandeered my living space.

Carol produced an auxiliary cord from god knew where and hooked her phone to my stereo to play music. She lay on the floor of the living room and thumbed at the phone's screen continually. Occasionally she would take a photo of herself, type something into her phone, or read us insulting messages in broken English she received on one of her many social networking accounts.

Her music was awful. My ears were assaulted with the sound of screechy girls whining about how'd they'd been wronged by all the men in their lives which was absurd because, by the pitch of their voices, they might have only recently hit puberty.

Horace read aloud from websites claiming cunnilingus cured cancer and gave tips on how to tell if a woman had an orgasm or faked it. I sat in my recliner and stared at the ceiling and wished a meteor would hit my house.

Horace said, "Did your wife get off every time?"

Carol's attention broke from her phone. "I have multiple orgasms every time."

"Did I ask you?" Horace said. "Abe, did Beverly get off every time?"

I continued to stare at the ceiling. "That's a personal question and doesn't warrant a response."

Carol said, "I bet she was frigid."

I turned my gaze to Carol. "You're a snot-nosed cunt. You think you're better than other women but I bet you're jealous of them and any attention they receive."

She gasped. "I'm not jealous of other women. Most of *them* are jealous of my open sexuality and beauty." She rolled around on the floor. She struck centerfold poses and began making snow angels.

Horace said, "You look like a lame cow."

Carol gave him an affronted look. I couldn't help but laugh. I couldn't remember the last time I'd laughed and it felt good. It also made me feel guilty. Beverly's passing made my life a joyless void where it was sacrilege to perceive anything as enjoyable ever again. Fun was a betrayal to her memory and our existence together. I stifled the laughter.

Horace said, "It's good to see you can find something amusing."

I shrugged and fought a smile.

Carol sighed, rolled onto her stomach, and propped herself up by her elbows. "I'm bored . . . and hungry."

"Let's go to the bar," Horace said.

I said, "Yeah. Why don't you guys go to the bar?"

Horace fumed. "You think locking me out is going to keep me from getting in the house? You're not getting out of going to the ceremony!"

"You can't break into my house. I'll—"

"We're leaving tomorrow morning for Virginia whether you like it or not! I'll drag you out of this house kicking and screaming if I have to!"

I stood and started toward the kitchen. "This is stupid."

"Where are you going?" Horace said.

I stopped in the kitchen doorway and turned to face him. "I'm gonna walk to the police station since your car is blocking mine. I'm going to tell them I've had two trespassers holding me hostage for the past twenty-four hours."

Carol said, "Can I come? I'm really hungry."

"I don't fucking care!" I shouted. "I want you both out of my house!"

Horace pointed his finger at me. "Less than five minutes ago you were laughing. *Laughing*, Abe. You've been pissing and moaning about how depressed you are and I've been trying to drag your ass out of this . . ." he waved his hand to insinuate the house, "morose house you call a home and show you Beverly being gone isn't the end of the world." He dropped his hand and his eyes rested on a photo of Beverly hanging on the wall. "For fuck sake!" Horace leaped out of his chair and snatched the photo off the wall.

"Put it back!" I took a step toward him.

He lifted the frame above his head. "Stop or I'll fucking smash it!"

I skidded to a stop.

Carol scuttled toward the sofa and out of the path of the possible projectile. "You're a lunatic!"

He lowered the photo and held it in front of his chest.

"All I'm asking is a couple of days away from this." He shook the picture. "And quit being such a fucking sad sack! Where's the guy I used to know?"

I said, "I'm pretty sure he was buried nine months ago."

"Let me take you to Virginia," he said.

Beverly's smiling face stared at me. I could feel emotion and tears lingering in the back of my throat. Horace lifted an eyebrow and slowly began to raise the photo above his head. I suppressed the loss and loneliness and replaced it with anger.

"Stop," I said. "I'll go."

Carol squealed. She jumped up and began to dance around the living room. A feeling of dread washed through me and made my anus clench as I thought about Carol coming with us.

Horace still held the photo above his head. "And you'll have a couple of beers with me."

I said, "Now come on—"

He lifted the photo above his head, a corner of the frame nicking the ceiling. He screamed, "Have a beer with me!"

Carol yipped in surprise at Horace's outburst. She collapsed on the sofa in a fit of giggles.

I held up my hands in surrender. "All right! All right!"

Horace beamed. He returned Beverly's portrait back to its spot.

"Goddamn it," I said. "Do you always have to shout?"

"I have to get your attention somehow."

Carol whined, "I'm hungry."

"You're always hungry," Horace retorted.

The two bickered as we left the house. Carol whined

about the ten minute walk and wanted to drive. Horace told her he couldn't afford another DUI. She pointed out he drove drunk yesterday. The nonstop back and forth was driving me insane and I was already regretting the trip. I walked faster to put some distance between me and them but Carol's voice was at such a pitch I was sure I would hear her a mile away.

I led them to a bar and grill close to the busiest intersection in town. Sometimes the place was overrun with bikers. They weren't the scary type of bikers you think of from movies. These guys were loud and obnoxious family men with too much money to spend on a superfluous vehicle they only rode six months out of the year. I wasn't sure why someone in Ohio would bother with such a vehicle. The weather was schizophrenic and would shift from nice to unpredicted thunderstorms in a second. The bikers brought their haggard and sun beaten wives along with them, or more likely their wives nagged them to ride to the 'little hippie town with all the tie-dye stuff for sale', and they rode around town when it was above fifty degrees and sat at stoplights and stop signs and revved the engines of their machines as if they were challenging someone to a race or justifying how much of a douchebag they were by bothering the residents with their excessive volume. If they hadn't dumped the money on a motorcycle they would have bought one of those enormous trucks with oversized wheels and a loud exhaust so they could peacock their manliness with a flashy and discordant object. I didn't know which vehicle was worse. The trucks were fewer in number but around all year long. The motorcycles came in packs during the warmer months. I was never sure what the lure was for them to come all the way to Yellow

Springs.

Fortunately it was a weekday. Most of the out-of-towners invaded during the weekend. We entered through the bar which was ill lit and it took a few seconds for my eyes to adjust. The bar was occupied by a single bartender with long curly hair who was conversing with a bloated redheaded man with dreadlocks. Their attention was trained on a recorded music concert playing on the large television hanging above the bar. The singer on the TV had black hair teased into a crazy mass, wore tons of black eyeliner and red lipstick, and was wearing some sort of giant black sheet. It took a few seconds for me to register the singer was a haggard old man and not a woman as we waited by the podium for a host to arrive.

In my peripheral I noticed Carol fidgeting and it dawned on me slowly she was dancing to the music coming from the television. Horace wandered over to a chalkboard with a list of beers on tap and began to complain they should've written the alcohol content beside each beer.

A woman in a patchwork dress with long salt and pepper hair appeared behind the podium. "Are you dining with us?"

I said, "Yes."

"How many?"

"Three."

She retrieved three menus from somewhere within the podium. Horace and Carol stopped what they were doing and joined me.

The hostess said, "Do you want to eat in the dining room or outside on the patio?"

"The patio," Horace replied. "So I can smoke."

The hostess gave him a forced smile and led us through the dining area. The dining area was home to a smaller bar with no attendant. There were two sets of patrons in the room. My attention was drawn to an overweight woman who appeared depressed. She chewed her food slowly and stared at a ten- or eleven-year-old boy she was dining with. The boy stared at his food with a blank expression and neither of them spoke to the other. A teenage couple sat a few tables away. The girl talked loudly about what posters were hanging on the wall of her room while her partner said nothing.

Our hostess led us through the glass doors to the patio which was filled with empty tables and chairs. She directed us to a small square table with four chairs near a reeking trash can inhabited by a couple of fat wasps flying lazily around the push in lid. We took our seats. Carol and Horace sat across from each other and I was forced to sit beside both of them. The hostess handed us our menus and told us a server would be with us shortly.

Horace retrieved a cigarette and lit it.

"I don't think you're allowed to smoke out here," I said.

Horace blew the smoke away from me. "What do ya mean? We're outside aren't we?"

"Do you see an ash tray?"

He waved his hand dismissively. "Who cares?"

Carol said, "Give me a cigarette."

"Support your own habit," Horace said.

She huffed, sat back in her chair, and folded her arms over her sagging breasts. She looked like a sulking child.

A male waiter opened the door and approached us with three sets of silverware wrapped in paper napkins. He had a loping gait and swung one leg in a rigid manner. He wore shorts which exposed the reason for his unusual stride. One of his legs was a metal prosthetic. Dread flooded me. I knew there was no way we would make it through the service without Horace saying something stupid to this unfortunate young man.

It was apparent the gears were whirling inside Horace's head. I shook my head minutely but he was too fixated on the waiter to acknowledge me.

The waiter stood between me and Carol. He placed the silverware bundles in front of each of us and pulled a notepad and pen from his pocket. "My name's Corey and I'll be your server today. Can I start you off with some drinks?"

Horace said, "What beer do you have with the highest alcohol content?"

The waiter peered up in thought and tapped the pen against his lower lip. "Dragon's Milk is pretty high."

"A pitcher of it," Horace said.

The server jotted the order down. "Three glasses?"

I said 'no' and Horace said 'two glasses' at the same time.

"I would like a glass of water," I said.

Carol leaned toward Corey in a suggestive manner and spoke in a sultry tone, "I'll have sex on the beach."

Corey gave her an uneasy smile. "I'm sorry ma'am. I'm not sure if we have that. I'll check with the bartender."

Horace laughed and said, "Ma'am."

Corey said, "Is there something else you want if they're unable to make your drink?"

"Um." She bit her lip. "A rum and Coke?"

He pocketed the notebook. "I'll be back with your

drinks."

Corey made his way back inside the bar. Horace never took his eyes of the man's metal leg as he left.

Once the door was closed Horace blurted, "Oh my god! Did you see his leg? He's a cyborg!"

"Shh," I said. "He might hear you."

"Who cares? It's not like he doesn't know he's a freak."

Carol chimed in. "I think it's sexy. I bet it's like having sex with the Terminator. He probably fucks like a machine."

Nervous someone would overhear our conversation, I said, "Can we talk about something else?"

Carol produced her phone from in between her tits. "I wonder if he'd let me take a selfie with his leg." She fiddled with the phone. "The selfie group would get a kick out of that."

"Selfie group?" I said.

"Yeah. I'm in a selfie group on Facebook."

I processed what she was telling me and all I came up with was absurdity.

She interpreted my silence as confusion and talked to me slowly as if explaining something to a child. "There are online groups with a particular interest. The group I'm in only posts selfies. Photos you take of yourself. The other people can comment or like the photo you post."

I said, "I get the gist of it. It doesn't make any sense to me though."

"Nothing makes sense to you," Horace said.

Carol gave me confused look. "What do you mean?"

"Well," I said, "taking a lot of photos of yourself is a narcissistic thing to do. If you have a bunch of people posting those types of photos, ultimately each person is *only* going to be interested in the results from their own photo and not pay any attention to the other photos. The fact it's a group would make you all groupies." I directed my attention to my menu and flipped through it nonchalantly. "Narcissistic groupies. Doesn't that defeat the purpose? It's not really a selfie."

"The photo is called a selfie," she said. "Because you're taking a photo of yourself."

"I know," I said. "But a selfie group is an oxymoron."

"I'm not a moron."

I sighed and looked at Horace for some guidance.

Carol stared at me blankly and tried to process what I'd said. It was apparent she was stumped for a comeback or argument. Her argument could have done nothing more than cement how vapid she was. Horace laughed. Her face fell into an expression of embarrassment. I wasn't sure if she was embarrassed because she realized how idiotic her group and their agenda was or if her chagrin came from someone trumping her with an intelligent explanation for her behavior. I was sure it was the latter. And what did it matter? She was too dull and dimwitted to allow an obvious revelation to change her behavior, because the things she did made her feel wanted, and taking that sensation away from a constant attention whore would be like taking away the air she breathed. She would have no more purpose in life.

"Buck up, troll," Horace said.

"Fuck you," she said. She lifted her phone and took a photo of Horace.

"Don't take my photo!"

She showed us the photo she'd taken of Horace's disgruntled face. "I'm posting it to the selfie group." She typed away on her phone with a self-satisfied smile.

Horace reached across the table and tried to take her phone. She wiggled in her chair like a child playing a game of keep away.

The door to the bar opened and their attention turned to Corey carrying the drink tray. I ignored the waiter and continued to search through the menu. He placed the pitcher in the middle of the table, gave Horace and I an empty glass, set a glass of water in front of me, and handed Carol a brown mixture.

Corey said, "The bartender wasn't sure how to make your drink. Here's a complimentary rum and Coke. Sorry for the inconvenience."

"Oh, thank you," Carol said.

"Are you guys ready to order?" Corey said. "Or do you need a few more minutes?"

"I know what I want," I said.

The other two feverishly searched their menus.

Horace said, "I'll have the Seaworthy sandwich and chips. Can I get the fish unbattered?"

"Sorry," Corey said, "I think we get the fish already battered."

Horace frowned. "I'll have the fish and chips," he repeated.

Corey turned to Carol.

She said, "The Reuben. With fries."

"And for you?" Corey asked me.

"BLT with fries."

"All right," Corey said. He collected our menus and left us again.

Horace poured both of us a glass of beer from the pitcher. Carol returned her attention to her phone.

"So," Horace said. "What are you going to say to Dr. Wiwi when you see him?"

I shrugged. "I don't know. I don't plan things. I think I'm going to return the cassettes I have and change my number when I get back."

"Why didn't you change it before?"

"Because I wasn't getting many calls and I was getting paid. It wasn't a big deal."

He took a drink of his beer. "The guy sounds like a douchebag and a scam artist."

I picked up my beer and smelled it. I took a tentative drink. The beer was bitter and almost made me gag. Horace laughed at me.

I said, "This stuff is disgusting."

"It'll put hair on your chest."

"I'm not drinking it." I set the beer close to him. "You can have it."

He slid the glass back toward me. "You promised to drink with me."

"I don't understand what drinking is going to accomplish."

"One beer. That's all I'm asking."

I sighed, lifted the beer, and took another drink. The second taste was as gross as the first. I suppressed a gag and imagined it would taste better after a few more swallows.

"You could have picked something lighter," I said.

"Stop complaining!" he shouted. "Drink your beer and lighten up. Forget you're the only person who exists in your pathetic little universe for one day and have some fun. You're a fucking monk! Quit depriving yourself of fun! Tomorrow we're driving to Virginia and having the time of our lives. And Saturday you're going to shove some cassettes up Dr. Wiwi's ass!"

"It's not going to be that dramatic."

"It should be."

Carol chimed in without looking up from her phone. "Life should be full of drama."

I said, "I hate drama. I prefer when things go as planned. I hate stress and problems and yelling and screaming and crying."

"How fucking old are you?" Horace said. "Life doesn't go as planned. Jesus, where the fuck have you been? Beverly is dead. Did you plan that?"

"No. That's not—"

"Who cares? Are you seriously going to drive all the way to the awards ceremony with a box of tapes, walk up to the guy, and timidly hand them over and be like," he pouted his lips and spoke in a child's voice, "here's your tapes mister." He furrowed his brow. "Fuck that guy! You only live once and you're not getting any younger. You need to fuck shit up."

"I suppose."

"I suppose," he mocked me.

"I'll figure it out when I get there. Quit pressuring me."

He held his hands up in a gesture of surrender. The three of us drank in silence. The third and fourth drinks of my beer were no less bitter but I grew accustomed to the taste.

Horace finished his beer. I still had half a glass. He produced his phone and began reading me titles of absurd news articles and made me watch a video clip on a loop of some guy getting hit by a truck. The patio door opened and Corey brought us our meals. Carol shoved her phone back into her cleavage. Before Corey could leave Carol ordered another drink and Horace requested another pitcher. I was almost finished with my first glass of beer and was starting to feel inebriated. I drank my water with my meal and Corey brought more drinks. Horace's vocal volume increased with each beer he consumed. I tried to decline a second beer but he made me feel guilty for not indulging on his dollar. I knew I would have a hangover in the morning if I continued to drink. The beer was stronger than anything I'd ever had and after two beers I felt like I'd consumed more than a six pack. I found myself laughing at Carol and Horace's argumentative exchanges instead of being annoyed with them and decided indulging in some alcohol wasn't so bad.

We bantered and drank and I began to notice more people entering the bar. A few people gave us perplexed looks as Horace became more animated. Horace paid for our dinner and bought another pitcher of beer. The sun began to set. I drank another beer and possibly another. I lost track of the number of drinks and time began to melt away as the three of us discussed and debated society and the next generation and politics and the trip ahead of us. The hostess seated other groups around us and they were served food and beer. Before I knew it the sky was dark and we were surrounded by people. The patio was alive with conversation and laughter and cigarette smoke and the stench of beer. Horace chain smoked and Carol bummed cigarettes from him.

At some point I became distracted and lost interest in the chatter at my table. I turned my attention to the young people around us. Most of them appeared to be in their twenties. They all had a carefree quality to them and I felt a ping of loss and desire for my youth. I became fixated on an attractive young woman with short purple hair who laughed with a man at a table nearby. I wondered if they were dating or friends or siblings. They looked like life hadn't beaten them down yet. And I wondered what the hell I'd done with my life. Why hadn't I done something more? Why did I choose to become a family man instead of a bachelor who went to bars and hung out with other young people and partied every night? Why, at the age of sixty-five, was I so miserable? I should've been happy I'd made it this far. Age was no longer the badge of honor it used to be.

A massive sound from inside the bar interrupted everyone's conversations and people began to migrate toward it. Carol squealed with delight and jumped up to join them. I stood and almost toppled my chair. I'd had too much to drink. Horace held me by the elbow and ushered me inside with the crowd since I was finding it difficult to walk.

A band played inside the bar and the volume made it difficult to talk. The pounding of the drums screwed with my equilibrium. I held a glass of the Dragon's Milk even though I couldn't remember bringing it with me. I drank it eagerly. Carol wiggled and danced with the younger people and the lights flashed and changed colors to the beat of the music. The music and beer and lights made me dizzy and I leaned heavily on Horace. He said something I couldn't hear and laughed loudly in my ear. Carol danced up to us and began to grind up against me. Horace gave me a slight push to make me stand on my own. The room spun with music and lights and Carol wiggled and jiggled in front of me. She faced me and I could smell her sweat and all the other unclean bodies around me and my stomach was uneasy. Without any prompt or warning Carol removed her shirt with a flourish and swung it in a circle above her head and screamed 'woooo'. She wasn't wearing a bra and the nipples of her stretched out and veiny tits pointed at the floor. I projectile vomited all over her chest as the song ended. The fountain of food and brown beer slid down her chest and splattered on the floor. The people around us made disgusted sounds and gave us a wide berth. Horace grabbed my arm and quickly ushered me out of the bar. Carol followed us, screaming like a banshee. She repeatedly smacked me and Horace yelled at her to put her top on before she was arrested for indecent exposure. I tripped over my own feet but Horace kept me from falling. I blacked out at some point and was never sure how I made it home.

8

Irregular banging and clanging of metal on metal woke me. I lay in my bed fully clothed. Dust motes floated lazily in the sunlight. There was an odd phantom pressure behind my left eye and tension in the back of my neck. I closed my eyes and tried to muster the energy to get out of bed. The moment I sat up the pressure behind my eye turned into a stabbing pain and shot over the top of my skull and down my neck. I was hung over.

Horace and Carol bickered in the kitchen as one or both of them rifled through the cabinets. I wanted to go back to sleep but knew I was going to have to move, take aspirin, and eat something before the effects of last night would subside.

Nausea struck. Pain pulsed from my eye to my neck. I shut my eyes, clutched the top of my head, and groaned. My stomach rolled and I suppressed a dry heave. I made my way to the restroom, still feeling slightly intoxicated, and Horace announced I was alive. I barely got the restroom door shut before I began to dry heave into the sink. I held onto the vanity to keep from collapsing onto the floor.

Horace and Carol laughed in the kitchen. I wasn't sure if they were entertained by my discomfort or amusing themselves. I didn't care either way.

I heaved again and the convulsion caused me to fart. Nothing was regurgitated for all my effort. Something did shift in my gut and my stomach rumbled. I drank handfuls of water from the faucet and took two aspirin from the medicine cabinet. The urge to defecate struck me suddenly. I clenched my buttocks and unfastened my pants as quickly as my shaky hands would allow. I dropped my pants and underwear and sat on the toilet just in time for my colon to explode. The smell made me gag. I closed my eyes against the pain in my head. I pushed my withered penis down with my hand to urinate while I sat there and only produced a pathetic trickle. I was dehydrated.

Once I was done I used a massive amount of tissue paper to clean myself. I flushed multiple times to keep the toilet from clogging since Yellow Springs had the shittiest water pressure I'd ever experienced.

I was certain at this point the two idiots in the kitchen were amused with the audio of my discomfort. I washed my hands and brushed my teeth, skipping my tongue for fear I would finally vomit. I splashed some water on my face since I'd begun to sweat profusely and drank from the faucet.

My stomach was battered and I was certain I was on the verge of death when I exited the restroom. The scent of coffee and something sweet assaulted me. I headed toward the kitchen. I stopped at the door and watched as Horace and Carol dipped pieces of French toast into a bowl filled with expensive maple syrup and ate with their bare hands. They spilled syrup on the counter and it ran down their hands. They both licked their fingers and wiped their hands on their shirts instead of using a paper towel or napkin.

Horace noticed me standing in the doorway. "Hey! There he is!"

The pain pulsed in my head with each syllable he shouted. I rubbed my forehead and said, "Please don't shout. I might vomit."

Carol stuffed her mouth with another piece of French toast and spoke with her mouth full. "I'm surprised you'd have anything left to vomit." She raised an eyebrow in a contemptuous expression and continued to eat.

Horace said, "Oh my god." He pointed at Carol while holding a piece of the toast. "You yacked all over her last night."

"Yeah," I said. "Sorry about that."

Carol shrugged as if it wasn't a big deal but I could clearly see it was. She dipped a piece of toast she'd already taken a bite out of into the bowl of syrup. I made a mental note not to eat any of the syrup. God knew what kind of diseases populated her mouth and I didn't think either one of them brought a toothbrush with them.

I picked up a piece of the toast and tentatively took a bite. The bread was soggy and undercooked and had an unusual texture. I gagged when I swallowed the slimy bread.

Horace said, "You're out of eggs. We dipped the bread in milk, cinnamon, and sugar."

I nodded and continued to eat. I waited until I'd eaten

two pieces before I attempted to drink any coffee. I poured the coffee and was hit with the overwhelming scent of vomit and spent cigarettes. Horace and Carol stank and needed to shower. I took my mug to the living room and sipped the bitter brew and waited for them to finish gorging themselves. My headache slowly subsided.

Horace leaned his head though the kitchen door. "You ready to hit the road soon?"

"I'm not going anywhere until we all shower. You guys smell of sick and smoke and if I'm enclosed in a car with you for more than five minutes I'm going to puke."

Carol made a disgruntled noise in the kitchen out of my line of sight.

Horace turned to her. "Wash your nasty ass."

"Fuck you," she retorted.

"You can stay here then," he responded.

She whined. "But I want to go."

He waved a hand at her dismissively. "Wash, skank."

She stomped off toward the restroom and slammed the door. A minute later shower sounds emanated from the restroom. Horace poured himself a cup of coffee and wandered through the living room and out the back door. He stood on the patio and smoked a cigarette.

I finished my coffee and went to my bedroom. I found an old duffle bag in the closet and packed it with enough clothes for two days. The back door opened and Horace called for me. I carried the bag into the office and dropped it on the desk. I called to Horace and told him I was in the office. I pulled the dusty box of Dr. Wiwi's cassette tapes from the top shelf of the closet. I set them on my desk.

Horace entered and pawed through the cassettes. "These them?"

"Yeah."

He selected one of the tapes and inspected it. He read the title from the paper jacket as if he were a commercial announcer. "'Dr. Wiwi's subliminal self-esteem booster! Improve your confidence while you sleep! If this tape doesn't boost your self-esteem in three weeks we'll give you your money back!'" He laughed and held up the tape for me to see the cover. "'Money back guarantee!'" He squinted and read the small flap on the back of the cassette. "'Check out all of Dr. Wiwi's subliminal tapes and change your life.'" He tossed the tape back into the box. "How many problems do people have that they'd get the whole set?" He shuffled through the tapes. "Insomnia, overeating, smoking cessation. Oh! This one is for you." He held up a cassette for depression, laughed, and dropped it back in the box.

"It's all garbage," I said.

"Doesn't look like you always thought so."

"It was a paycheck."

"That's your problem. You can't sell trinkets if you don't have faith in them."

"I don't sell them. I wait for them to call me because they want to buy them. I'll be glad to give them back and change my number."

"What are you gonna do for a job?"

"Don't need one. I did this for extra cash because Beverly wanted to travel. I'm fine with my retirement. Besides, I'll get social security in a couple of months when I turn sixty-six."

The bathroom door opened and Carol joined us. Her hair was dripping wet and her odor morphed into something reminding me of a wet dog. She had no other clothes than the ones she'd arrived in and I was sure they were the source of her stench now. I almost offered her some of Beverly's clothes but knew they wouldn't fit and didn't know if I could stomach the mental trauma of this woman wearing my deceased wife's clothes.

Carol reached for one of the cassettes. "Can I have one of these?" She grabbed a random tape and read the cover.

I picked up the box and held it away from her. "No. I'm returning *all* of them." I repositioned the box under one arm and tried to snatch the cassette from her hand.

Carol twisted away from me while keeping her eyes on the tape's cover. "Just a minute," she said. "I'm looking at it."

Horace said, "Don't bother. All the self-help tapes in the world couldn't fix you."

"Fuck you," she said. "I don't need any help. There's nothing wrong with me."

"Really?" he said. "Could've fooled me."

She put a hand on her hip and gave him an incredulous look. She waved the tape in his face. "You only have issues if you believe you have them."

He laughed. "Oh no. You definitely have issues. You just haven't been properly diagnosed by a professional. And I don't think Abe has any tapes to help with personality disorders."

"Whatever," she said and headed toward the living room with the cassette.

I made a mental note to retrieve it from her before I returned the box. I figured it could be equal to dangling a shiny object in front of an infant's face. It would keep her occupied for a while. Possibly long enough for me to regain my sanity.

"I'm going to shower. Do you want to take your stuff to my car?"

"Sure," I said.

Horace lifted my duffle bag and we proceeded to his car. He fished his keys out of his pocket and unlocked the trunk. The smell of hot garbage and mildew assaulted me once he opened the door. I fought the urge to gag again. My stomach was still in a state of unease from last night's excursion. I peeked into his trunk to find the source of the smell. His trunk was littered with clothes.

I shifted the box in my hands. "What's all this?"

He tossed my duffle bag on top of the heap of clothes. "Sometimes I don't get a chance to go home in between screwing dames. When my clothes get awful, which . . ." he lifted his arm and sniffed his armpit, "these are getting ripe, I buy a new set and throw the nasty ones in here."

"You don't wash them?"

"I don't have time for that! Actually . . ." He scooped up an armload of the soiled garments. The action stirred the rank smell of sweat and booze and cigarette smoke. "Where's your trash?"

I leaned away from him and held my breath. I shook my head, took a couple steps back, and almost dropped the box of cassettes in my hasty retreat. "Jesus, they smell like death. Why don't you wash them? Throwing them away is wasteful."

"I don't have time to wash clothes! That's women's work! Where's your trash?!"

"You don't know how to do laundry, do you?"

Horace became enraged and threw the clothes on the ground. He frantically began to collect more clothes and add them to the growing pile.

"Come on, Horace. Don't throw that shit in my yard!"

"I don't have time for this! I don't have time for laundry! I'm a very busy man!"

"Don't get pissed at me because I found one of your flaws."

"I'm not flawed! I'm too busy!"

I tilted my head toward the side of the house. "The trash cans are around the corner. Stop throwing them on the ground!"

He ignored me and continued to unload all the foul clothing until the trunk was empty except for my duffle bag. I sighed and set the box of cassettes by my bag. Horace closed the lid, ignored the enormous mess he'd made, and went inside without another word to me.

I observed the neighborhood and wondered if anyone witnessed Horace's temper tantrum. I didn't see anyone outside or peeking through their windows. I walked to the side of the house, retrieved a trash can, and wheeled it to the pile of clothes. Holding my breath, I cleaned up Horace's mess.

9

Horace pulled into the drive of a small geodesic dome. The house was located at the end of a dead end street. It was on a street in my town I'd never traveled down. He put the car in park and killed the engine.

The house was constructed out of concrete with large pieces of colorful glass set into the walls. A crude crescent moon was carved above the door. The home was nearly obscured by the overgrown foliage surrounding it. The grass needed mowing a month ago and the flowerbeds were overtaken with weeds.

Horace said, "Hurry up. We don't have all day."

Carol shifted in the back seat.

I said, "This is your house?"

She flung open the back door. "Yeah. Why?"

I shrugged, not taking my eyes off the house. "I've never seen a geodesic home in person. I had no clue there was one in town."

"Maybe if you got out more, instead of being self-involved, you would've noticed it."

Horace turned to her. "Would you hurry up so we can go?!"

Most of the effects of last night's drinking were gone but the volume of Horace's voice inside the car made my head throb. Carol, now pissed at Horace, exited the car and slammed the door. I closed my eyes and rubbed my temples.

After a few seconds of quiet Horace said, "We're leaving her."

I opened my eyes. "What?"

"Fuck her. She's a cunt. This trip is for bros only."

Carol stomped up the overgrown cobblestone walkway.

I checked to see if she'd left anything in the back. The cassette she'd taken from the box and her cell phone lay on the seat. I grabbed both of them. We watched as Carol produced a key from between her breasts, unlocked the door, and disappeared inside. I set the cassette in the console between us.

Carol was inside her house for approximately ten seconds when Horace started the car. He backed out of the driveway and I rolled down the window. He shifted into drive, cranked the wheel, and punched the gas. He misjudged the space he'd needed to turn and hadn't pulled out of the drive far enough. My hand was out the window to throw Carol's phone when the passenger door mirror clipped Carol's mail box. The metal on metal was as loud as a gun blast and scared me.

The fright made my chest hurt. I yelled, "Watch out, fucking idiot!"

Horace drove into Carol's yard and howled with laughter. I threw her phone toward the door of the house and it landed in an overgrown flowerbed. Horace attempted a half-assed doughnut but the grass was too thick. He gave up after a bit and steered the car back toward the road.

"God damn it! You're gonna get us arrested!"

As we pulled onto the road the front door flew open. Carol ran out onto the steps and screamed something unintelligible.

Horace said, "Time to go."

I shouted to Carol, "Your phone is in the flower bed!" I pointed in the direction the phone landed.

Horace punched the gas and the wheels screamed in protest on the asphalt. He whooped as the car fishtailed before it regained traction and shot down the road.

Carol screamed, "Don't leave me!"

I adjusted the mangled side mirror and caught the reflection of Carol running after us. She gave up the chase after she realized it was pointless.

And we were on the road to Covington, Virginia.

10

Horace drove to the grocery store parking lot in Yellow Springs and parked. He retrieved his phone from his back pocket and typed something on the screen.

"What are you doing?" I asked.

Without taking his eyes off his phone he said, "I don't know where we're going. Jeeps is going tell us."

"Jeeps?"

"GPS."

"Oh."

A female voice emanated from the phone's tiny speakers informing us to head north on Walnut Street. Horace propped up the phone in a nook on the dash near the odometer.

He asked, "Which way is north?"

I pointed in the direction of the ice cream stand.

He retrieved a battered pack of cigarettes from his pants pocket and lit one. "We need some beats," he said.

He blew cigarette smoke out the window and stuck the cigarette in his mouth. He tilted his head, squinted against the wafting smoke, and reached for a worn cord dangling from the cassette player of his outdated stereo. He noticed the cassette in the console, picked it up, and began to peel the plastic from the case.

I said, "Hey! Hey! What are you doing?" and tried to snatch the cassette back.

Horace twisted from me. "Stop it!" He held the tape near his window, took the cigarette from his lips, and held it like a menacing weapon. "I'll burn you!"

I leaned away from him. "You're a psychopath!"

"I want to listen to it."

"You have to pay—"

"I'm not paying for shit! Fuck that guy! We're gonna shove all these tapes up his ass!"

"Because violence solves everything."

"Sometimes it's the only way to get through to people."

"We are not going to Virginia to fight someone."

"Why not?!"

"Because it's barbaric and illegal."

"Illegal! Who says?"

"The law."

He managed to tear half the plastic from the cassette.

"God damn it, Horace! You've ruined it!" I sighed and sat back in my seat. "Might as well listen to it since it'll probably come out of my last paycheck."

He placed the cigarette back in his mouth and removed the rest of the wrapper from the cassette. The smoke from his cigarette drifted toward me and I told him to put his window down. He complied and his phone simultaneously made a soft ding and vibrated against the dash. He squinted at the screen and ejected a cassette from the radio. A wire with a headphone adapter was connected to the tape.

Horace cursed and picked up his phone.

"What?" I said.

"Carol." He typed something and placed the phone back on the dash. "I told her to fuck off and die and blocked her."

"Blocked her?"

"So she can't contact me anymore."

"You can do that?"

"Yeah." He popped open the cassette case and put the tape in the player. "Let's get going." He drove in the direction I pointed.

Dr. Wiwi's voice filled the car. "Welcome to Dr. Wiwi's subliminal self-help tape to build confidence. This tape should be played while sleeping to allow the phrases to become part of your subconscious."

The female voice of Horace's phone interrupted with directions. He made a right turn at the Corner Cone. The day was warm and bright and there were a decent amount of people gathered in a line at the ice cream stand. Once we turned the corner I spotted a young couple dressed like they'd stepped out of the sixties standing outside a small shop that sold marijuana smoking supplies.

"Let's begin," Dr. WiWi said.

Horace stared at the couple as he stopped at the intersection. "We should get some pot."

"I am confident," Dr. Wiwi said. "I grow more confident every day. People like me."

The phone announced more directions.

I said, "We're not smoking pot."

"I am attractive," Dr. Wiwi said. "I can do anything I set my mind to. I believe in myself."

"Why not?" Horace said.

I said, "Because we're responsible adults."

"Overrated." He followed the directions the phone announced.

The cassette continued. "I am comfortable with myself. I am respected by my peer group. I can take control of any situation."

Horace drove down the main road and out of town. Dr. Wiwi's voice continued to list off phrases to build our confidence: I am confident in social situations, I always speak my mind, I effortlessly start conversations with strangers, etc. After twelve phrases the list of commands started over again. We made our way through the countryside listening to the cassette and I became drowsy. Somewhere near Clifton I hit the button to eject the tape and tossed it out the window.

"What did you do that for?!" Horace shouted.

"I'm tired and I don't want to fall asleep while that shit is playing."

"It could do you some good to listen to those."

"I'm fine being miserable."

He pushed the cassette with the wire attached back into the tape deck and fumbled with the wire to plug it into his phone while driving. Once the cord was attached he thumbed the screen a few times until some god awful music began to play. He rocked in his seat animatedly and grinned at me.

"Jesus. What the hell are we listening to?" I said.

"'Two Princes'!" he shouted. "The Spin Doctors!"

"It's horrible. Turn it down so I can sleep."

I turned toward the door and let the seat down.

"Come on!" Horace shouted. "We're bros on an adventure!"

I shouted, "Sleep!" and put one arm over my head to cover one ear. I inserted a finger into my other ear to block out the racket.

Horace said something else but I couldn't make it out. I knew he'd leave me alone after a bit. And he did. Once the first song was finished he turned the volume down. I slept fitfully while he drove. I woke now and then when his phone announced directions through the car speakers, interrupting the song it was playing.

11

I willed myself to sleep as much as possible to pass time. I pretended to be asleep when I was awake so I wouldn't have to carry on a conversation with Horace. Time felt endless, feigning sleep, and I lost track of it. After a bit I decided to straighten my seat up and take in the surroundings.

The first thing I spotted was a McDonald's billboard with a photo of a sausage McGriddle, super-sized French fries, and a large chocolate milk shake with a slogan boasting you could now purchase the items any time of the day.

"This is what America has come to." I waved my hand to insinuate the sign.

Horace said, "What?" He peered up at the sign as we passed it. "Breakfast anytime is a fantastic idea. Especially after a long night of drinking. It's better than Waffle House! You don't have to get out of the car. Waffle House needs a drive-up window!"

"Not the breakfast anytime. Did you see the same billboard I did? A sugar-coated breakfast sandwich, deep fried potatoes, and a copious amount of mushy ice cream in a cup. What about that is a healthy meal? It goes to show the world is run by the consumers and what they want. The whole while experts are banging their heads against the wall and screaming there's an obesity epidemic. Maybe the consumer shouldn't have it their way."

"That's Burger King."

"What?"

"Have it your way. Burger King."

I shook my head, leaned my seat back, and closed my eyes. Feigning sleep was the best option. I was getting burnt out on Horace. Most of our hang outs ended in pointless squabbles and one of us leaving unceremoniously.

After an eternity of Horace's terrible music and faking sleep the car came to a stop. Horace killed the engine. I put my seat up and found we were at a gas station.

"Where are we?"

"Nitro." He fished his wallet from his back pocket.

"I know. What town?"

"The name of the town is Nitro. We're in West Virginia. We need gas. If you need to piss you'd better go. Jeeps says we've got two and a half hours left."

He exited the car and went through the usual rigmarole of filling the car with gas. I got out and stretched. My body was stiff from being in the car.

The gas station was surrounded by large concrete buildings. Most of the structures were missing windows and had layers of peeling paint. Even the gas station appeared run down. We were the only car at the pumps. A greasy-haired teen peered out the window at us and I didn't see any customers inside. I moseyed into the station store. The clerk watched me suspiciously. The restroom sign was suspended from the ceiling past the checkout counter and down a filthy hallway. There were two doors for the restrooms. I opened the door for the men's and the sickly light from the hallway shone on a single toilet and sink. I tried the switch but the light didn't work. I leaned out of the doorway and found the clerk watching Horace intently as he filled the car.

I said, "Hey! The light doesn't work."

The clerk turned to me with an open-mouthed expression. "Kay."

I waited a beat for him to move from his position and rectify the problem. He stayed seated and stared at me.

"Are you gonna fix it?" I said.

"Cain't leave the register unattended."

I briefly debated asking permission to use the women's restroom or proceeding without asking. But it struck me the clerk must've had to use the restroom himself at some point in the day. He had to be aware the light was out and was too lazy or incompetent to fix it. The clerk was young and from a generation unable to take responsibility for anything. Everyone expected the next person to be the one to do something but the next person had the same policy and in the end nothing got done until someone with an ounce of common courtesy or ambition got frustrated with the situation or sick of everyone's apathy and took it upon themselves to do something.

I entered the darkened restroom and stepped in front of the sink. The door closed behind me and I didn't bother locking it. I unzipped my pants and proceeded to relieve myself in the direction I thought the toilet was situated. I could hear my urine splattering against either the wall, floor, or side of the toilet. Wherever it landed wasn't in the toilet bowl. When I finished I turned toward the sink, washed my hands blindly, and didn't dry them since I didn't want to fumble in the darkness to find the towels, touching every filthy square inch of the restroom in the process. I slung the water from my hands and exited the restroom. Horace was standing in the hallway waiting his turn.

"I wouldn't use this one," I said.

"Why not?"

The clerk lingered behind the counter, nosily watching us with an expression of idiocy.

I whispered, "The light doesn't work and I pissed on the floor."

Horace sniggered in a conspiratorial fashion and pushed past me to enter the men's room. I whispered for him to be careful not to step in it and proceeded to the coolers in the back of the store. The refrigerators housing the drinks smelled like rotten food when I opened the door and none of the drinks were cold. I decided water would be the safest bet. I collected a couple bottles, walked the aisles, and found a couple of granola bars. I took the items to the checkout. The clerk rang up the items. I paid him and realized I was left with less than fifty cents to my name. A battered ATM sat beside the door but I didn't trust it. Everything in the store either wasn't in working order or covered in a layer of neglect. I made a mental note to find an ATM once we were situated at the hotel.

Horace emerged from the restroom with an evil grin. I held up the water and granola bars to convey the message I had purchased something for him to eat and drink. We both headed for the car.

Horace barked a laugh when he started the car. "I pissed in the sink!"

"What a lazy little shit," I said. "How fucking hard is it to change a bulb? I'm sick of the whole apathetic generation. I don't get it. They're either completely uncaring and unwilling to do anything or crippled by their offended sensibilities. I'm convinced they're the product of their parents' overconsumption of anti-depressants. Apathy is a plague."

"Maybe next time he'll learn," he said. Horace maneuvered the car out of the gas station lot and followed his phone's orders to the highway.

"That's the thing. He won't learn. They never do. You could give them all a list of directions and explain why if they follow it their life will be easy and happy but they'll stare at you with a vacant look and toss it in the trash as soon as you walk away."

Horace took the ramp back to the highway. "Are you finally admitting you're an angry old man?"

"Yes. Yes I am." I counted the items off on my fingers. "I find the younger generations stupid and lazy. I couldn't tell you the name of a single popular band or song. Whenever I see a magazine at a checkout counter with a celebrity face on the cover I think to myself, 'Who the fuck is that?'" I dropped my hands. "I've lost my grip on reality. The world is foreign to me. It feels like I've traveled through time and found myself in an era where everything has changed and I haven't changed with it because I was suddenly dropped into a foreign land. But I've been here the whole time. I've watched it all change around me and I've stayed the same. And another year passes and each fad that sweeps through the population makes a new alternate reality. I find each one more absurd than the previous one. It makes me feel as if I'm going crazy because no one else notices it or they *do* notice it but they don't care."

I opened my water bottle and took a drink. My mouth was disgusting from sleeping in the car and I swished the water around before swallowing it.

"I think you need to relax," he said. "You can't change the world and you *will* make yourself crazy. What you need to do is cut loose and maybe find a dame to take your mind off things."

I capped the water. "It hasn't been a year since Beverly died! Just because you don't have any self-respect or respect for the deceased doesn't mean the rest of the world doesn't!"

Horace waved his hand at me dismissively and fumbled with his phone. His awful music filled the car again. I concentrated on the scenery of the rolling mountains and lush trees to ignore him. Ten minutes later we entered Charleston. The highway was carved into the mountain and elevated over the city. I'd never been to Charleston but for it being the capitol of the state it was rundown and depressing. The most interesting thing was a large building with a gold dome. Horace told me it was the capitol building. He said the gold was real. I thought the money could've been used for something more useful to the residents. From the highway the whole city looked like a giant scrapyard.

We passed through Charleston without incident and continued on the West Virginia Turnpike. Horace chain smoked and I was happy the weather was decent enough to put down my window so the smoke didn't give me a headache. A bright yellow sign announced we were approaching a two dollar toll both.

"Fuck!" Horace said. "Do you have any cash?"

"I have some change."

"How much?"

I dug the loose change from my pocket. "I don't know." I fingered the coins and counted them. "I have forty-seven cents."

He slapped the steering wheel. "Damn it!"

"You don't have any money?" I searched the console and floorboards for any loose change.

"I don't carry cash! I always use debit or credit!"

"How do you go through life without real money?"

"It's real money!"

"Stop shouting!"

"What do I do?!"

I spotted a sign announcing it was the last exit before the toll as we were passing the exit. "I guess we could've gotten off there and found an ATM."

"Fuck!" He slammed the heel of his hand against the steering wheel.

"Calm down. We'll figure something out. What can they do to us if we don't have—"

"They'll arrest us!"

"That seems extreme for two dollars."

"They have to take a debit card, right? It's the future. Everyone takes debit! What kind of business wouldn't take debit?"

"Technically I don't think it's the future. Today is the present. Tomorrow is the future."

"Stop fucking with me! Oh my god! There's the toll! I don't know what to do!"

The highway split into several lanes with booths. Horace slowed the car. Other vehicles zipped past us and got into a lane. Some of the booths had overhead signs marked 'cash only' and two lanes had signs with the words 'E-Z Pass' in italics.

"Maybe you should take the E-Z Pass." I pointed at the lanes filled with semi-trucks.

"We don't have an E-Z Pass!"

"What's an E-Z Pass?"

"It's a prepaid toll card."

"Why don't you have one of those?"

"Why don't *you* have one?! Because I don't pass through a hundred tolls on the West Virginia Turnpike every day, asshole!"

"Would you calm down?"

Horace slowed the car to a crawl. An impatient driver behind us honked. He flipped them the bird and screamed a line of profanities. The driver flew around us. A small child in the back seat flipped us off as they passed.

Impatiently I waved my hand at a cash lane. "Just get in line. Try to use your debit card before we get in an accident."

Horace steered the car into the lane with the least amount of cars. He mumbled to himself in a state of panic and kept repeating we were going to jail. He became more and more agitated as each car in front of us paid their toll and was given a green light to proceed.

"There's no arm," he said. "Maybe I should drive through without stopping."

"If you drive off we *will* get arrested."

There was one car between us and the booth. Horace fished his wallet out of his back pocket and slipped his debit card from its home. The car in front of us zipped off to join the other traffic merging back onto the highway.

Horace advanced our car and smiled at the frumpy and apathetic middle-aged woman seated on a stool in front of a register. She chewed a piece of gum open-mouthed and held out her hand. She wore a blue latex glove.

The woman said, "Two dollars."

Horace handed her his debit card. She looked at it, confused. In a one-handed fluid motion she slipped the card between her index and middle finger and extended it back to Horace.

"What's this?" she said.

"My debit card," he said.

"We only take cash."

He pointed at the card she still held out to him. "It's as good as cash."

The woman sighed heavily. "Sir, we only take cash."

He snatched the card back from her. "We don't have any cash."

I leaned forward to peer around Horace. "I have forty-seven cents."

"That's not two dollars," she said.

Horace said, "What do we do then?"

The woman rolled her eyes impatiently and slipped off her stool as if it took a great effort. She grabbed a pen and a note pad and slid open the metal door separating us from her. She walked behind our car and jotted something on her notepad. Horace and I turned to watch her. A long line of cars formed behind us. A few of the vehicles pulled out of the line and steered toward other booths where the procession wasn't being held up by two assholes who didn't have cash.

Horace said, "She's writing down my license plate

number! We're gonna get a ticket!"

The woman slowly made her way back into her booth and entered something on her register. The machine printed a slip. She handed the paper to Horace. He inspected it for a second.

"What's this?" he said.

The woman was becoming more impatient. "That's an unpaid toll ticket. You'll have fourteen days to pay the toll online before you get hit with a late penalty. Show it to any other tolls you pass and they'll add their fee to it."

"Oh," Horace said.

"Make sure to pay it before the fourteenth day. The late fees get pretty nasty." She waved at him to insinuate he should move along. "Please pull through, sir. There's a line behind you."

Horace placed the slip of paper in the console and laid his wallet on top of it before pulling away from the booth.

12

We passed a second toll booth and Horace collected another unpaid toll. Other than the
numerous amount of adult porn store bill-
boards and the beautiful scenery West Virginia didn't have
much going for it.

Horace exceeded the speed limit most of the trip and
we rolled into Covington before five P.M. The city emanated an awful stench similar to flatulence. The smell was
nearly gag inducing. Most of the buildings and houses
were run down and on the verge of being abandoned. And
there was an abundant amount of small churches.

The hotel was easy to find. Horace pointed out a gas
station within walking distance. He parked the car in the
small lot with room for fifteen cars. The hotel was small in
comparison to most other chain hotels I'd visited. We exited the car and stretched our limbs.

Horace said, "Jesus, this fucking city smells like a stale
cunt. What *is* that?"

I shrugged. "Maybe it's the river."

"What river?"

"The one we passed on the way in."

I walked to the back of the car and mimed for him to open the trunk. He produced his keys and unlocked the door. A residual odor of dirty laundry wafted from the trunk. I gathered my bag and the box of tapes.

We made our way to the front desk and found a young girl with her head bowed typing on her phone. She wore an unflattering green polo shirt with the hotel logo embroidered where a breast pocket should've been. She pocketed her phone once she was aware of our presence.

"Can I help you?" she said.

"Yeah," Horace said. "We have a reservation."

She placed her hands on the keyboard of a computer. "Name?"

"Horace Sherwin."

The girl typed something into the computer and asked for his driver's license and a form of payment. He retrieved his wallet and gave her the appropriate cards.

I observed the small lobby and spotted a handmade poster board sign propped on a rickety easel. The sign read 'Dr. Wiwi's Sales Award Ceremony' in gold glitter. The next day's date and the time of eight P.M. were hastily scrawled in black marker below the title. I elbowed Horace and pointed at the childish handmade sign. He stifled a laugh.

The girl behind the desk slid a paper toward Horace. "Sign this."

Horace signed the paper with a flourish.

The girl handed him two key cards. "You're on the third floor. Do you have any questions?"

"Yeah," Horace said. "Is there a Kohl's around here?"

The girl pursed her lips and appeared thoughtful. "I think there's a Kohl's in Roanoke."

"Where's that?"

"About an hour south."

"That's too far. Is there a high end fashion store in town? A Sears?"

I said, "Those aren't high end fashion stores."

The girl's eyes flicked to me and back to Horace. Her smile was forced. "There's a Walmart and a K-mart in town."

Horace shook his head. "What about JCPenney?"

She raised her eyebrow and shrugged in surrender. "I'm sorry, sir. We don't—"

"Gah! Does me no good."

Frustrated, he waved at her dismissively, turned, and headed toward the elevator. The girl looked to me apologetically.

I said, "I have a question. What's that smell outside?"

She said, "Westvaco. It's a paper mill."

I nodded and joined Horace at the elevator. He repeatedly pushed the button to retrieve the lift.

I said, "I don't think that's going to make it go any faster."

"I'm going to have to buy clothes from Walmart like a pedestrian!" He hit the button for the elevator harder.

"Buying clothes from Kohl's is pedestrian."

"No it's not! They have major name brands."

"There are major name brands everywhere. It doesn't mean the clothes are original or better. It's all mass produced no matter how much you pay—"

"You don't know anything about fashion! Look at

you," he waved his hand to insinuate my attire, "with your . . . dress pants and button down shirt. You look like you work in an office!"

I laughed. "Is that an insult?"

"Well . . . yeah."

The elevator doors opened and we entered. I was assaulted with a foul odor as we stepped into the box and the door slid shut. Horace's face screwed up in revulsion.

"God," he said, "it smells like a pile of dicks in here!"

"Calm down."

"It's fucking awful! Tell me you smell that."

"I smell it."

"My nose is being accosted!"

"Don't be so dramatic."

The doors opened. A woman stood in the hall and appeared surprised someone was in the elevator. She wore jeans and a T-shirt and looked to be in her early thirties. She was attractive even though her appearance was plain and nondescript. She held a pack of cigarettes and a lighter and her eyes were bloodshot and puffy as if she had been crying or sleeping.

Horace exited the elevator and said, "That smell isn't us."

The woman's glance bounced between the two of us, confused.

I shrugged and followed Horace. "Excuse my friend. He can't find a Kohl's."

The woman chuckled and entered the elevator.

Our room was a few doors from the elevator. Horace struggled with the key card for a minute before the door unlocked. Inside the door we found a standard hotel room with two beds, a television, a refrigerator, and microwave.

Horace flopped onto the bed nearest the window, pulled a charging cable from his pocket, and plugged his phone into an outlet located on the tableside lamp. He began to type on his screen. I entered the restroom, relieved myself, washed my hands, and joined him by sprawling out on the other bed. Horace played on his phone. He held the toll ticket with one hand and thumbed things into his screen. I grabbed the remote from the tableside and turned the television on.

I said, "Do you think that woman is here for the ceremony?"

He didn't look up from his phone. "Who?"

"The woman at the elevator."

"Maybe?" He was silent for a beat. "Jesus Christ! Those two tolls cost fourteen dollars because we didn't have any cash! That's criminal!"

"Do you think there's an ATM close?"

"Probably at the gas station."

I flipped through the channels as Horace grumbled about the ticket and presumably paid it on his phone. When he was finished he unplugged his phone.

He said, "I'm going to go to Walmart to get some clothes. Wanna come?"

"I don't want to go shopping with you."

"You could use some new clothes too."

"I'm fine. I packed a bag."

"We'll get dinner when I get back."

I read the clock beside my bed. "It's already a quarter till six."

"I won't be long. Need anything?"

"Nope."

I thumbed through some channels. He stopped in the

restroom before heading out. I mindlessly watched television while he was gone. The programming made me realize how long it had been since I'd actually sat down and watched television. The shows weren't what they used to be. Most of the channels were filled with shows about regular people with mental problems who yelled at their friends and family constantly about the most tedious things. The cameras followed them around as they went about their day: Cooking, cleaning, going to the BMV. Except for one show whose protagonist was a rich woman with an expressionless face and a monotone way of speaking which made me think she was either dead inside or heavily medicated. Her show was about her rich problems, which disgusted me.

The commercials baffled me the most. Almost every advertisement was for a medication with a very specific condition. I didn't see how the advertisements were relevant since I thought doctors prescribed medicine *only* if you were required to take it. It made me wonder if there was a pandemic of IBS and diabetes and shingles and incontinence and erectile dysfunction and Alzheimer's and circadian rhythm disorder and OIB. I didn't even know what OIB was but wondered if people were constantly shitting their pants with limp dicks and forgetting about it and it was causing them to lose sleep at night. In this day and age it wouldn't surprise me.

There was a commercial with a celebrity playing golf, complaining about blood clots. Some of the commercials had animated organs with faces and limbs. It depended on the condition and what organs were affected. The television showed a bladder shopping with an old woman and I thought, *Is this why a lot of older people constantly complain of health problems?* Any time I was out in public and passed older people talking I would catch snippets of their conversation. They mainly talked about what 'procedure' they'd recently had done or what medications they were on or what new diet their doctor prescribed. It made me sad to think this was all they had to talk about. People my age didn't have hobbies to occupy their free time. They had doctor's appointments instead.

The phone on the desk by the television rang and startled me from my reverie. The sound was something I had grown accustomed to not hearing and it confused me. Who knew we were staying here? And why were they calling? I didn't know if Horace told Carol which hotel we were staying at and the thought of talking to her filled me with dread.

I got out of bed and stared at the dingy yellow phone as it rang. The phone was an office phone. There were several buttons on the right-hand side in addition to the standard numbered buttons. A red button flashed when it rang. I answered the phone hesitantly and held the receiver to my ear and listened without saying anything. I could hear odd sounds on the other end but no one spoke.

"Hello?" I said.

Horace said, "Abe. Meet me out front of the hotel in five minutes."

I breathed a sigh of relief it wasn't Carol.

I said, "Why?"

"I found an Applebee's."

13

I exited the elevator and spotted an ATM in the hallway. I withdrew forty dollars and grumbled about the
outrageous bank fees. I had to agree to the fees in order to receive my cash. I despised ATMs. If I was forced
to pay a hostage fee to retrieve my money the machines
weren't as convenient as they advertised. I stuffed the
money and the receipt into my wallet and proceeded to the
main entrance.

The sun was almost down. Horace's car idled in the
turnaround. He was smoking a cigarette and playing with
his phone. I entered the passenger side. He had already
changed into the new clothes he'd purchased. I imagined
he must've done so in the bathroom of the store. But it
wouldn't have surprised me he'd changed in the parking
lot at the store.

He said, "What took you so long?"

"Found an ATM inside. I had to pay eight fucking dollars to get my money. That's a twenty percent penalty be-

cause my bank isn't in every town across the country. Why is it my fault the bank is incompetent and doesn't know how to run a business?"

"What ya need cash for?"

"We're going to eat."

He took a drag from his cigarette and the smoke garbled his voice. "Use your bank card."

"I prefer cash."

"What's your hang up on cash?"

"Could we go? I'm starving."

He shrugged and put the car in drive. We didn't speak much. His route put us back on the highway and we took the next exit. There were a couple of turns once we were off the highway. We passed a large shopping center with a Walmart as the focus. Horace followed the winding road. We passed all of the businesses and came upon two large warehouses on either side of the road. The area was abandoned and creepy in the dark. I started to wonder if Horace knew where he was going. I finally spotted the lonely restaurant beyond the warehouses at the end of the dead end street. The building was surrounded by trees and was an odd area for an eating establishment. It was almost as if the owners didn't want people to find it. Horace pulled into the small parking lot and found a spot. There were a handful of other cars and it didn't appear to be too busy.

I said, "What kind of food do they have?"

Horace tossed his cigarette out his window and gave me an incredulous look. "Don't tell me you've never ate at an Applebee's." He retrieved his phone from the dash and slipped it into his pocket.

I shook my head.

"Oh my god," Horace said. "I can't believe you've

never been to an Applebee's."

I opened my door and he did the same. We were parked behind the restaurant and I followed Horace toward the front. At the back of the building was a patio area lit dimly with hanging strands of Christmas lights and a tacky inflatable palm tree. From what I could see in the dim lighting there were also a few scattered tables and chairs. Two shadowy figures sat at one of the tables with a pitcher of beer. Both figures were smoking and one of them spoke loudly about someone named Joan and I thought he said something about her stealing his dick.

We entered the restaurant. Our hostess was an unattractive female with exceptionally crooked teeth. She asked if we were dining or wanted to sit at the bar. Horace told her we were eating but would like to sit close to the bar. She informed us the restaurant would close in an hour and the kitchen would shut down in thirty minutes. I wasn't sure if she was being rude and didn't want us there or if she didn't have the proper social courtesies needed to be a hostess. She showed us to a small, tall table with high barstools.

After I finished struggling to climb the tall chair and be seated I took a look around. There were several televisions mounted above the bar. All of the screens were airing the same baseball game and the volume of the game competed with the awful music the restaurant played. A group of five men sat at the bar together and stared at the televisions like zombies, a beer sitting in front of each of them.

A few tables away a heavily bearded man wore a shirt with the word 'ironic' screened on it. He sat with a girl wearing glasses too big for her face. Her shirt had the words 'corporate logo' across the chest. They both scowled and ate their food.

The group at the bar let loose a sudden cheer and startled me. The men half leapt up off their barstools with their hands thrown in the air. One of the men grabbed the back of his neighbor's neck and shook him. The scowling couple glanced at the rambunctious group, rolled their eyes, and conversed with one another with contemptuous expressions.

Horace said, "Isn't this great?"

"This is awful."

"What?!"

I wasn't sure if he was yelling because of my answer or because he truly couldn't hear me over the deafening music and television combo. A twentysomething waitress with an orange tan and long black hair pulled into a ponytail appeared with two menus. She dropped the menus on the table as if it exhausted her to lift her arms and gave us an open-mouthed and derisive look. She said something to me but I couldn't hear her. I politely asked her to repeat herself.

The waitress shouted, "Drinks!"

I said, "Water."

She turned to Horace with the same open-mouthed expression. I wondered if she'd had a stroke at some time and the constant state of derision was a side effect. I didn't think so. She was more than likely a bitch to everyone.

"A pitcher of beer!" Horace shouted.

She shouted, "What kind?!"

He waved at her dismissively. "Whatever has the highest alcohol content!"

She stared at him dumbfounded as if she didn't understand what he'd said.

Horace held up two fingers. "Two glasses!"

The waitress turned and slowly walked toward the bar. She dragged her feet in an unusual manner. She wore large white high-top tennis shoes with puffy tongues. Her laces were undone and appeared intentionally untied. Having loose shoe laces when your job was nothing but walking with your hands full was asinine. The waitress slipped behind the bar and began the routine of filling a pitcher from the tap but did so in slow motion. There didn't appear to be a bar attendant.

Horace looked around and spotted the scowling couple. He stared at them for longer than necessary. I busied myself with the menu.

The menu was filled with grease heavy options. I found a section labeled 'Lighter Fare' but the dishes were just smaller portions of the other items. The Lighter Fare section also boasted it was 'made a little better for you' but by the look of the sad selection the claim was a stretch. The Lighter Fare items were also the same price as their counterparts.

Horace leaned close to me and said, "How's a beard ironic? I don't get it."

I strained to hear him over the other commotion.

I said, "I don't know. Who has a beard ironically?"

He discretely pointed to the couple. I looked at them.

"Don't . . .!" He leaned away from me. "Don't look at them," he hissed.

He picked up his menu. The waitress approached with a platter housing the pitcher of beer, two glasses, and my water. She sat my glass down roughly. Water splashed onto the table. She sat the remaining items on the table in the same fashion.

When she was finished she said in an unfriendly tone, "Do you know what you want?"

Horace nodded.

I said, "Can I have the pepper-crusted sirloin?"

She didn't write my order down. "How do you want the steak?"

"Medium rare."

Horace said, "An order of cheeseburger eggrolls. And I'll have the quesadilla burger. Pink. With fries."

The group at the bar cheered and whooped again. The waitress left us unceremoniously. Horace poured a beer for each of us.

I said, "Whatever you ordered sounds like the most disgusting thing in the world."

"What?!"

I repeated myself but raised my voice for him to hear me.

He said, "You have to try the cheeseburger eggrolls! They're delicious!" He drank half of his beer in one swallow.

"Nothing about that sounds delicious," I said, "and you order like a pompous ass."

"How so?"

I put the emphasis on the first two words and mocked him. "*I'll have* the quesadilla burger."

"What's wrong with that?!"

"It sounds rude."

"Well, what the fuck should I say? I didn't bark at her to bring me a burger, bitch. There's nothing wrong with how I ordered!"

"It sounds more polite to say *can I get* or *can I have* like you're asking. Not *I'll have* like some sort of command."

"You're out of your head! It's a fucking burger!" He leaned toward me to whisper harshly and conspiratorially. "You know who's pompous?" He thumbed toward the couple. "The guy wearing the beard ironically."

"Just because his shirt says ironic doesn't mean his beard is ironic. You're the one out of his head if you think people grow facial hair to be ironic."

"He's mocking people who grow beards!"

I took a drink of my beer. "Wouldn't his shirt say sardonic instead?"

"You're splitting hairs over words?!"

"No one uses them correctly."

"Oh, Jesus Christ!" He leaned back in his chair. "Sometimes I think you want to quibble with me for no reason."

I shrugged and drank more beer. The men at the bar broke out in an argument over something that happened in the game on the television. The waitress reappeared with our appetizers and two small plates. She left us promptly and shuffled beyond the bar and slipped out a door to the outside. At first I thought she might be taking a cigarette break but she reappeared with an empty pitcher and refilled it at the bar. I'd forgotten about the patio area.

Horace pushed the eggrolls around on the plate with a fork and eventually stabbed one. He said, "You have to try one of these," and popped one into his mouth. He opened his mouth and panted. "Hot!"

I picked up my fork and cut one in half. A steaming and unappetizing mixture of meat and cheese spilled onto the plate. My stomach rumbled from hunger and the beer wasn't helping. I deliberated eating the disgusting egg roll, thinking it might make me vomit.

"No thanks," I said.

Horace stabbed another egg roll. He methodically worked his way through the plate until he'd eaten them all. The waitress appeared with our meals as he masticated the last egg roll. She set a small plate in front of me with a medium, not medium rare, steak. The steak was pre cut into strips as if I were a child and couldn't have managed this on my own. The meat lay on top a pile of watery vegetables and grains. Horace received a foul looking burger with a tortilla wrap as a bun. The waitress asked if we needed anything else and Horace told her another pitcher of beer.

We ate in silence. My food not only didn't look appetizing, it didn't taste good either. The men at the bar erupted into cheers or arguments periodically. The couple finished their meal, paid, and left. Horace kept vomiting a steady flow of banal banter. The waitress announced last call and the men at the bar groaned. Most of them ordered another. Horace and I nursed the rest of our pitcher.

The waitress brought us our bill ten minutes before closing time. Horace paid and we slipped out of the restaurant through the door leading to the patio. I was tipsy from the beer. Once we were outside Horace stopped on the patio to light a cigarette.

"Hey, buddy, can I buy a cigarette from you?"

The two people we'd seen on the way into the restaurant were still hanging around outside. They both approached us. The Christmas lights didn't illuminate the area well and I took a step back. Their approach made me nervous and I thought they might try to rob us.

Both of the men wore khaki pants. One of them wore a red and white striped shirt and held out money to Horace.

Horace looked at the bill the man held. "That's a twenty. I don't have change."

"Can I buy a cigarette from you?" the man said and shook the money.

Horace retrieved two cigarettes from his pack and held them out to the man. "Don't worry about it."

"Thanks!" the man said.

He took the cigarettes, handed one to his friend, and pocketed his money. The two lit their cigarettes but remained close to Horace and me. The men held their cigarettes in a strange fashion as if they weren't really smokers. They made me extremely nervous and Horace began to scrutinize them. Finally the one who'd asked for the cigarettes spoke.

"My name's Keith and this is Kevin." He thumbed to his companion. "We're not fags."

"Neither are we," Horace said.

Keith said, "Good. You guys look like you need to cut loose."

Kevin said, "We're going to Wild Times."

"What's that?" I said.

Keith said, "A bar."

Horace caught my uneasiness. "We have to get going." He dropped his cigarette and crushed it with his shoe.

I wasn't sure if it was the lighting but Kevin looked as though he were tearing up. Horace and I turned to leave. Kevin yelled at us once we were halfway to our car.

"That's okay! They don't let fags into Wild Times anyway!"

Horace grunted, spun, and stomped toward them. He was in fight mode. One of the two men shrieked and they stumbled over each other to rush inside.

Horace said, "I can't believe I let you smoke my cigarettes! You ungrateful fuckers!"

I chased after Horace and grabbed his arm. "Fuck those guys! You'll get arrested!"

He tried to pull his arm free of my grip. The darkness and alcohol threw my equilibrium off and Horace's jerk knocked me to the ground. My knee hit the asphalt and sent a shock of pain up my thigh. I yelped and Horace laughed at me.

I writhed on the ground, holding my knee. Small pieces of gravel bit into my ribs but I didn't care. The pain in my knee drowned out all other discomfort. Once the pain was manageable and Horace exhausted his humor at my misfortune I growled for him to help me up. He extended his hand and I took it. He pulled me to my feet and almost fell himself. I limped to the car.

The pain sobered me and throbbed as we drove back to the hotel. I recommended Horace stop somewhere to get more beer.

He stopped at a gas station near the hotel. I stayed in the car on account of my wounded knee. He returned a few minutes later with a case of warm beer and more cigarettes.

"Why didn't you buy something cold?" I said.

"They didn't have anything cold."

"What gas station doesn't have cold beer?"

"One in Virginia! We can get some ice out of the machine at the hotel and fill the bathroom sink. They'll be cold in ten minutes."

"Why do I get the feeling you've done this before?"

He smiled and started the car.

I said, "I'll need some ice for my knee."

We drove the quarter mile to the hotel. Horace carried the beer since my knee was killing me. He headed toward the front entrance. I followed him, limping.

The woman we'd passed at the elevator stood outside smoking by a bench. A cigarette extinguisher was located beside her. She stared at the screen of her phone forlornly. As we approached the entrance she noticed us. Her expression shifted to one of concern as she watched me limp and try to keep up with Horace.

Horace lifted the case of beer and said, "Beer in room 308!"

She smiled hesitantly and crushed her cigarette on the butt extinguisher. She slipped her cell phone into the back pocket of her jeans and strode toward us.

She said, "I could use one of those." She turned to me. "And by the looks of it, you too."

Up close I noted a few more wrinkles on her face than our first encounter. I put her age somewhere in the vicinity of my daughter's. She extended her hand to me to shake since Horace's hands were full. She had a tattoo on the palm of her hand but I couldn't make it out.

"Laura," she said.

"Abraham," I said. I thumbed to Horace. "This is Horace."

Horace said, "We're not rapists."

Laura said, "I should hope not. All I want is a beer and I'm pretty sure I could take both of your feeble asses." She eyed my knee. "Especially since one of you is lame."

A car drove by the front of the hotel with a man hanging out the passenger window. He shouted, "Everything you know is wrong!"

We all turned our attention to the car.

Laura said, nonchalantly, "Someone's having an existential crisis."

We all laughed.

Horace said, "Come on. Let's get this beer on ice!" He stepped in front of the motion detector for the door.

We entered the lobby and a greasy-faced man stood behind the check-in counter. He scrutinized us with a sour expression. The sign for the award ceremony still stood at the entrance to the small dining area attached to the lounge area.

I pointed to the sign as we headed toward the elevator and asked Laura, "Are you here for the awards?"

She looked over her shoulder at the sign and gave a derisive snort. "No," she said.

Horace said, "Business or pleasure?" He said pleasure in a lurid manner and watched her reaction eagerly.

I wanted to smack him. Laura was probably half his age. Even though there wasn't anything illegal about their age differences the thought of someone our age copulating with someone young enough to be their child was repulsive and felt pedophilic to me.

"Neither," she said. "I'm here for my mother's funeral."

I said, "I'm sorry."

"Why are you sorry?" she said. "We all die. Shit happens."

"You're dealing with it well."

She shrugged. "There's nothing I can do to bring her back. Wallowing in grief isn't going to help. Besides, I hadn't talked to her in a couple of years. I have a life of my own, you know."

We'd reached the elevator and Horace shifted the beer

under one arm in order for him to hit the button repeatedly. He inspected Laura's physique in a leering manner without her noticing.

I didn't know how to respond to Laura. I didn't know why I'd apologized to her when she'd said her mother died. Why did people apologize for things they didn't do? And she was right. She was an adult. The same way my children were adults. They weren't required to check in on me or talk to me every day or every week. They had lives of their own. And I'd had a life of my own when I was their age and didn't dote on my parents whenever they were lonely. We're all in this alone and that's an inevitable part of life no matter how you look at it.

The door for the elevator opened and we entered. I hit the button for the third floor and the doors shut.

Horace said, "What about your dad or other family? Why aren't you staying with them?"

She shrugged. "They're kinda assholes. I can sleep in and have my own small private sanctuary here."

I couldn't argue with her. When Beverly died all I wanted was to be left alone. The kids stuck around for a week but they were emotionally needy. I wasn't equipped to deal with them. I wasn't going to lie and tell them it was okay and it was going to get better. It wasn't. I knew all of our lives changed drastically in the blink of an eye and I couldn't help them. I battled with my own loss. And I couldn't understand why Tara and Nathan couldn't see I wasn't even able to help myself. There was nothing I could do for them. But this was the world now. Everyone was concerned about themselves and to hell with anyone who couldn't fulfill their needs.

The elevator doors opened and we made our way to the

room. Once inside Horace placed the beer in the bathroom sink. I sat on my bed and rolled up my pant leg to look at my knee. There was a large purple bruise on my swollen kneecap. Horace shouted we needed ice and Laura grabbed the ice bucket to fill. I pointed to the sanitary plastic bag inside and asked her to fill it for my knee. Laura left and Horace exited the restroom with a can of the warm beer. He opened it and took a drink. He stood a few feet in front of me. He stared at my knee for a few seconds, nursing his beer, and shook his head.

He said, "The real question is . . . you or me?"

"What?" I said.

"Are you tagging her? Or me?"

I took a deep breath and let it out slowly. "You're a sad sad sad pathetic little man."

"What?!"

"I don't have the energy to explain how fucked up you are. Not just fucked up but fucked up on every level a person can be."

He pointed his index finger at me with the hand holding his beer. "Who the fuck do you think you are to judge me?!"

I yelled, "Her mother just died, you fucking prick! Her mother who's the same fucking age as you! It would be like fucking her dad!"

He stepped forward and shoved my shoulder. I almost fell back on the bed.

"Keep your dick mitts off me!" I said.

"Fuck you! Just because your wife's dead and you're too sad to get a stiffy doesn't mean I can't have a good time!" He chugged the last of his beer.

"Come on," I said. "She'll be back any minute. Don't

be a raging asshole. Her mom died. She wants a beer. Let her have a moment without trying to put your penis inside her."

He belched. "Whatever." He tossed the empty can into the trash and went to retrieve another.

There was a knock on the door. Horace let Laura in. She carried two buckets of ice and the plastic bag, all full of ice. She said she'd gone ahead and grabbed the bucket from her room too. Laura dumped both containers over the beer in the sink and emerged from the bathroom with the bag of ice wrapped in a washcloth and handed it to me. Horace flopped on his bed and began to sulk. He turned the television on and flipped through the channels while he drank. Laura sat in the chair for the desk.

Laura and I talked about nothing and everything. The usual conversation. Where are you from? What do you do? I told her about the award ceremony and she told me she thought the sign in the lobby was a joke. Horace periodically interrupted us and asked Laura invasive questions. She wasn't bothered by them and brushed him off. He interrupted her constantly. After a bit she retrieved a beer for herself and brought me one. Our conversation continued as we all drank. Horace told Laura my wife was dead but the information didn't bother her. We breezed over the topic and moved on. Horace was the only one bothered by our dead family members and tried to bring it up periodically. His level of drunkenness made him forgetful and he kept repeating himself. After a couple beers the ice I held to my knee was melted and my knee didn't feel as stiff.

The next thing I knew the clock on the night stand read three A.M. and the beer was gone. Talking with Laura was organic and I'd wished I was able to talk to my kids in the same unrestrained fashion. The two of us shared a common bond in death but neither of us wanted to dwell on it and neither of us wanted to beg for sympathy from the other. We knew from experience it was something each person dealt with in their own way.

Laura thanked us for the beer and the conversation. Against Horace's protests she retreated to her own room. When she was gone Horace opened the window and lit a cigarette. I told him I didn't think it was a smoking room. He grumbled and said he was paying for the room. He used a spent beer can as an ashtray.

The beer made me sleepy. Horace didn't protest when I shut the lights and the television off. I slipped into bed. The streetlights silhouetted Horace in the window. He smoked and I tried to think about what I was going to say to Dr. Wiwi tomorrow.

14

Our room door opened. In a state of panic I jumped out of bed. I thought one of the house-keepers was entering to clean while we were sleeping. But no one entered and the door was shut. It took me a few seconds to notice Horace's bed was empty.

Once the panic and confusion subsided I became aware of my sore knee. The pain wasn't as terrible as last night but it wasn't something I could ignore either. I retrieved my bag and dumped it on the bed. I dug through my belongings until I found aspirin. I dry swallowed two tablets and made my way to the bathroom. I took a long hot shower and inspected the large purple bruise on my knee. The swelling was gone and there wasn't any major damage other than the bruise.

I exited the bathroom and found Horace sprawled out on his bed. He was accompanied by a smorgasbord of breakfast food. He had several paper plates scattered around him. All of them were loaded with muffins, bagels, and fruit.

He said, "They don't have a proper breakfast here. It's one of those stupid do-it-your-damn-self places."

I picked up a banana and searched for drinks he might have commandeered but didn't see any.

I said, "Do you want some toilet coffee?"

"Huh?"

I thumbed over my shoulder. "There's a coffee maker on the vanity in the bathroom. It's probably covered in ten thousand people's shit particles." I peeled the banana and took a bite.

"I think it's a stretch to think ten thousand people have stayed in this room. Maybe ten. I don't understand why this hotel exists. This town doesn't even have a Kohl's! What town doesn't have a Kohl's?!"

I shrugged and grabbed a muffin from one of the paper plates. I sat at the desk to eat.

He took a bite of a bagel and spoke with his mouth full. "What are we doing today?"

"I don't want to do anything."

He chewed the bagel and swallowed it. "What do you mean? We're on vacation! We have to do something!"

"You just said there's nothing here. And I'm not in the mood to go sightseeing. This isn't a vacation for me. I wanna return the tapes to Dr. Wiwi and go home—"

"You're not going to sit in this room until eight o'clock like a sad sack! You came all the way here to return tapes? You could've mailed them to the guy."

"Are you senile?! You're the one who forced me to come!"

"Oh yeah," he said. He waved at me dismissively. "Forget it. I'm bored."

"You can't force me to have fun."

He shouted, "Fucking Christ! You could at least act like my friend and fucking amuse me!"

"All right! Would you quit shouting?!"

"I'm not!"

Horace's phone made a noise. He pulled it from his pocket and thumbed the screen. I finished the banana and threw the peel in the garbage. He continued to type into his phone while I ate my muffin.

Horace said, "There's a bar on Madison."

"I'm not going to a bar."

"Why not?"

I checked the time on the clock beside the bed. "Because it's ten o'clock in the morning. I don't think they're open . . . what the hell time did you get up this morning? Jesus. I swear you're the only person I know who can drink like a fish, sleep two hours, and be ready to go to the bar when you wake up."

He continued to play with his phone. "There's nothing else to do around here."

"There has to be. Find something that doesn't involve alcohol."

"TripAdvisor's number one suggestion is Humpback Bridge."

"What's that? Code for a gay hangout?"

Horace laughed. "No. It's an old historical bridge and park."

He turned the screen of the phone toward me and extended his arm for me to see a photo of a wooden covered bridge. I leaned forward in my chair and squinted at the photo. He pulled the phone back and touched the screen with his thumb a couple of times.

"There are only five things on the list," he said. "The bridge, a waterfall, a lake, a scenic trail along a river, and . . ." He moved his thumb over the screen, waited a beat, and laughed. "Red Zone Sports Bar!"

"Bodies of water or beer," I said. "I guess I pick the bridge. I don't know if my knee will take hiking around water. Are you sure there aren't some museums?"

He shook his head, not taking his eyes from the screen of his phone. "There's a railway museum about an hour away."

"I don't understand why Dr. Wiwi would have an award ceremony here. It's a shit hole. There's nothing to do—"

"He doesn't even have the decency to rent a hall."

"Because the lobby is free."

"The hotel has to charge him something."

I shrugged. "We haven't seen another person who's attending the damn thing. Maybe I'm the only sales representative. None of this makes sense." I looked at the box of cassettes sitting on the floor. "I should give the cassettes to someone at the front desk and tell them to hand them over. This place sucks. Let's go home."

"No! We can't go home!"

"Why not?"

"Because we're on an adventure! I want to meet Dr. Wiwi!"

"What if the guy is violent? What if I give back the tapes and tell him I quit and he punches me in the face?"

"You're creating worst case scenarios to get out of something you don't want to do. Grow a pair! What do you have to lose?"

"I don't have anything left—"

"Quit being a Dougie Downer! You've got your kids and sanity."

"My kids have their own lives and my sanity is paper thin."

"God!" He threw himself back on the bed. A muffin rolled off one of the plates. "I have to get out of this room! You're depressing as fuck! I can't talk to you!"

"All right. All right! We'll go to your damn humping bridge!"

Horace laughed and sat up.

I said, "I could use some open space."

We ate the array of sugar loaded food he'd pilfered. Horace flipped through the television stations aimlessly while he ate.

Once we finished our breakfast we headed to the car. I assumed at some point we might run into another guest here for the ceremony. The hallways were empty except for cleaning carts and the only person at the check-in desk was a hotel employee.

Outside smelled like a wet paper sack filled with farts. The sky was cloudless and bright. Horace navigated us to the bridge using his phone. We took the four lane highway to a narrow two lane highway with no shoulder. The shoulder of the road had a guardrail. And a guardrail was a requirement because the road was carved into the mountain and there was a steep drop off the mountain inches from the road. I wondered how anyone got around here in the winter time. I would be afraid of sliding off the side of the mountain. Eventually the drop became less harrowing and disappeared. The land leveled out into a grassy field and railroad tracks materialized alongside the road.

Horace's phone announced our next turn and he took a

narrow, single lane road. We passed under a bridge supporting the train tracks and the old wooden bridge was directly on our left. The bridge was covered and arched, hence the name. Past the bridge was an empty parking lot with a tiny grassy area home to a couple weather-beaten picnic tables. Horace parked and killed the engine. We both stared at the bridge.

Sarcastically, I said, "Wow. This looks exciting."

"Maybe it *is* a gay hangout."

We exited the car and moseyed toward the bridge. The path leading into the bridge had a handrail and I took advantage of it. My knee didn't hurt but it didn't feel stable. I took slow and deliberate steps and, surprisingly, Horace didn't give me any flack about my speed. The bridge was long and the inside was dark and ominous. A small square of light shone bright at the end.

I stopped at the end of the bridge and peered down at the stream running beneath it. The water was clear and I could see the rocky bottom. A couple of small fish swam lazily in the slow current. The water wasn't more than a trickle and some of the rocky bottom was exposed.

A plaque was mounted at the entrance of the bridge. Horace approached it.

He read aloud, "Humpback Bridge. Constructed of hand hewn timbers in 1835 for the James River Kanawha Turnpike Corporation. Remained in public use until 1929."

He went on to read the bridge was reconditioned in 1953 from the effort of fundraising by local businesses and in 1954 the bridge was dedicated as a memorial to the pioneer spirit of this country. I laughed once he finished. Horace shot me a confused look.

I said, "Fuck this bridge."

"What did it do to you?"

I shook my head. "Nothing. Why'd they bother fixing the damn thing?" I waved my hand toward the empty parking lot. "No one gives a shit about this bridge. They used to give a shit about it when they needed it. But not—"

"I give a shit about this bridge!"

"No you don't!"

"It's a historical landmark!"

I pointed at the plaque. "Who built it?"

"It doesn't say—"

"Because no cares!" I poked the plaque rapidly. "Someone designed this bridge. A group of people built this bridge. Where are their names?"

He shrugged.

"Exactly!" I waved my hands frantically. "Don't celebrate the people who made it. Celebrate the people for restoring it. But it still doesn't matter. It'll all be flushed down the toilet of history. The people who built this bridge are as forgotten as the fucking bridge itself."

"It's just a damn bridge!"

"I hate it. It used to have a purpose but now . . . it's worshipped for existing."

Horace shook his head, mumbled something, and walked into the darkness of the bridge. I followed him. I was astonished how dark it was once inside. Horace stopped halfway across and I almost ran into him. I could barely discern the silhouette of him.

He said, "This place is almost two-hundred years old and you don't feel anything for it."

"I'm sixty-five and no one feels anything for me."

We were still. The sound of birds and trees rustling in

the wind and the faint trickle of the water below echoed faintly and eerily through the bridge.

I whispered, "I thought there would be more."

"More what?"

"Life or . . . something. I don't know. I thought there would be more to life. I remember thinking I would become successful somehow when I was young. I was hopeful for the future then. But now I realize my younger self was a parody of what I'd become as an adult. I wanted more out of life. I wanted my life to have meaning. I didn't think Beverly would die before me, ya know? I feel lost."

"I think that's normal."

"I've been lost my entire life because I've been hoping for something that doesn't exist. It took until I had to be my own company before I realized it. When you're alone it gives you too much time to analyze the choices you've made. It's like thinking of the perfect comeback after you've walked away from a conflict."

The sound of him scuffing his shoe on the ground startled me. He cleared his throat. The conversation made him uncomfortable. But there was comfort and a degree of anonymity in the darkness. We both knew the seriousness and brutal honesty would remain here when we left. We didn't have to tell the other not to mention this conversation again. We were men talking about weak emotions. We were raised to suppress those things.

He said, "We're all lost."

I shook my head even though I wasn't sure he could see me. I said, "How do you do it?"

"Do what?"

"You don't act as though life has beaten you down. In

fact, you always seem happy as a lark."

"I have to keep myself occupied. Because if I stop . . . if I have to face myself and the silence and everything I have and haven't accomplished I feel lost too. Everyone does. And it's terrifying if you stop to think about it. To think we're all alone. Everyone has to fill the aloneness with other people and hobbies and kids and television and music and food and marriage and fucking and vacations and whatever will distract them from the emptiness. If they didn't and took the time to see how meaningless it all is they'd probably kill themselves."

A breeze ran through the bridge and caused the hair on the back of my neck to rise. I shivered.

"Come on," he said. "I know your knee is bum but let's look at the waterfall."

I followed him back to the car. I thought about how we hadn't crossed the bridge to the other side. If the moment were a work of fiction there would be something allegorical here. But this was life. And life was full of anomalous moments you couldn't break down and interpret without driving yourself crazy. You had to keep moving forward.

15

The outlook for the waterfall was beautiful. The sky was clear and the mountains were endless.

Horace snapped photos with his phone. He fiddled with the screen and flipped it toward me and said, "This looks better."

The photo he'd taken of the waterfall was worn and faded.

I said, "That's not a good photo. The lighting is weird."

"What?!" He inspected the photo. "There's nothing wrong with it! It's Instagram! It's supposed to make your photos look old."

He did something with the phone and showed me the same image. The lighting was normal in the photo and showed the majestic beauty of nature.

I said, "Why would you want the photo to look that way? People who took photos fifty years ago didn't intend for them to end up looking like shit. They wanted to capture the essence of what they were experiencing so they could remember it in vivid detail years later. Or when they showed their friends and family they could see what they saw. In a year when you look at that photo," I pointed at his phone, "you're going say to yourself 'this isn't how I remember it' but that's how you'll remember it because you won't have a true photo."

He showed me the screen and swiped his finger back and forth across the screen to show me both images. "The app stores both images in my phone."

I waved my hand at him dismissively and said, "Forget it." I didn't have the energy to argue with him.

A family arrived at the base of the waterfall: a man, a woman, and three elementary age children. The children removed their clothing to reveal swim suits beneath and plunged into the water. Their screams and laughter echoed through the trees.

"Let's go," I said.

"Why?"

"Because we look like creeps watching other people swim."

"Gah! It's not like we're up here jerking off and watching them!"

"Still . . ."

"All right!"

"Stop shouting."

"I'm not shouting!"

The woman below turned her head in our direction. I took my leave and Horace followed.

Once we were to the car Horace complained he was hungry and needed to get another change of clothes for the ceremony. We stopped at a gas station and raided the aisles for chips. I found a display of old slices of pizza under a heat lamp. We both bought two slices of the stale, questionable pizza, a snack size bag of chips, and water. Horace added a forty ounce bottle of beer to his purchase.

He drove to the Walmart parking lot. Once we were parked I retrieved the napkins I pillaged from the gas station. I laid a few of them across my lap. Horace watched me, confused. I balanced the flimsy cardboard box of pizza in my lap.

He said, "You're wasting napkins."

"I don't want to get pizza grease on my pants."

I opened the pizza box and poured my chips into the lid.

Horace opened his pizza and set it on the dash. He twisted the top off his beer and drank a good portion of it. He lifted the pizza out of the box, took a bite, and a thick dab of sauce dropped onto his thigh. I pointed at the sauce as if to say 'see'.

He shrugged his shoulders and spoke with his mouth full. "That's why we're at Walmart." He swallowed his food. "You could use some new clothes too."

I was wearing a blue short-sleeve button down shirt and gray slacks. I said, "There's nothing wrong with my clothes."

"Are you wearing *that* to the ceremony?"

"Yeah. Why?"

"Oh god. You look like an office worker! It's a ceremony!"

"They didn't say it was a formal affair."

"You should always dress nice. You never know when you're going to meet a broad."

"I'm not concerned with—"

"You should let me buy you an outfit."

"You? Dress me?"

"Yeah."

"I don't think so."

"Why not?!"

"Because I don't want to look like a desperate old man trying to be hip."

"I'm not a desperate old man trying to be hip!"

"You look like one."

Horace took an angry bite of his pizza and chugged half of his beer.

I said, "One of these days I'd like to take you on a sober tour of your insecurities."

With his mouth full he said, "Fuck you! I'm not insecure!"

I ignored him and continued to consume my pizza. We watched the Walmart shoppers enter and leave the store.

Halfway through my second piece of pizza I said, "This is sad."

"I know," he said. "How can someone let themselves go like that?"

He was gazing out the windshield. His eyes followed a large man trudging across the parking lot. He was having trouble walking due to his massive girth.

"Not him," I said. "This." I raised the last bite of my pizza. "Eating in the car. It's barbaric and pathetic. We should be sitting at a table with proper eating utensils like civilized human beings."

Horace didn't respond. I finished my food. Horace drank the remainder of his beer and stated he was ready. I debated if I should stay in the car. I didn't know how long he would take and thought it would be more entertaining to roam the store.

Something felt off as we approached the store. The people exiting stared at us for a few seconds longer than what I would consider socially kosher. I couldn't place their expressions. Some of them radiated disgust.

Once we entered the store Horace headed straight toward the men's department. I followed him reluctantly and couldn't help but notice a few more people watching us with brazen interest.

Horace stopped at a table full of men's button down shirts sealed in plastic bags. He lifted a lavender one and read the size on the collar tag. He held the bag under his chin and turned to me.

"What do you think?" he said. "Does purple look okay?"

"I don't know. It's purple. It's a lady's shirt."

He flipped the package over to look at the shirt front again.

He said, "It's a man's shirt."

"The color doesn't look like a man's shirt. Purple is for ladies."

"Not anymore it's not!"

A man in a camouflage baseball cap pushed a shopping cart past us. A small boy sat in the cart and prattled to his inattentive father. The man stopped ten feet from us and flipped through a rack of NASCAR t-shirts. His child begged for some candy and he ignored the boy's pleas. The man eyed us dubiously and it made me uncomfortable.

I whispered, "Don't shout."

"I'm not shouting. There's nothing wrong with this shirt."

"Okay. There's nothing wrong with it."

He lifted another shirt the same color. "You should get one."

"There's nothing wrong with my clothes."

"It's an award ceremony! You should look nice." He wagged the packaged shirt at me. "There might be hot chicks."

I snatched the shirt from him and threw it down on the table. "I'm not wearing a girl's shirt. Stop hassling—"

"All right! Stop rampaging!"

"Can we go?"

"No. I need dress pants and a tie."

I sighed. He took a few steps and stopped in front of an endcap with a myriad of neck ties. He pulled a plain black satin tie from the rack. He craned his neck until he spotted the dress slacks. The pants were folded and shoved into cubbyholes on a shelf near the man with the child. Horace pawed through the slacks until he found what he wanted. He unfolded a pair of black trousers with two sets of deep pleats and held them by the waistband to his own waist.

He said, "How do these look?"

I wanted to tell him they were ridiculous but instead I said, "They're fine. Are you done?"

"Stop being whiney."

"I'm not whining."

"Oh!" He spotted something and rushed toward it.

A shelf beside the man and child housed several different fedoras. Horace lifted one with a rhinestone design and placed it on his head.

He said, "I've wanted to get one of these." He tilted it forward. "Is it me?"

The man flipping through the shirts stopped abruptly. He stared at Horace with an expression halfway between mortified and angry. He took the handle of his cart.

The man muttered, "Faggots," in a thick southern accent as he left.

The child said, "Where's faggots, Daddy?"

Horace did a double take. "Did that motherfucker call me a faggot?!"

I said, "Yeah."

Horace removed the hat from his head and shouted, "Fuck that redneck!"

The man continued out of the men's department without flinching. But Horace's shout had drawn the attention of other shoppers and they didn't look happy.

I said, "I think it's time to go."

"Yeah! Fuck these backwoods bumpkins!"

"Would you keep it down? You're going to get us lynched."

"I don't care!"

I grabbed his arm, spun him around, and pushed him toward the registers. He protested loudly and I reminded him he'd been drinking and the last thing he wanted was to get arrested in a redneck infested town for public intoxication. He gave up the fight reluctantly and proceeded to the self-checkout lane.

Horace scanned each item and placed them in a bag as the computer instructed. I'd never used a self-checkout and didn't understand the concept. A frumpy woman in her thirties leaned against a podium and watched us suspiciously. Horace retrieved his wallet, produced a bank card, and slid it through the reader.

I asked, "Do you get a discount for doing it yourself?"

"What?" Horace said.

I motioned to the machine and his bag. "You're doing

the work of the employees. Ringing it up and bagging. The store is saving money by not paying an employee. You should get a discount for saving the company money."

Horace blinked at me as the machine spit out a receipt and reminded him to remove his items from the bagging area.

"No," Horace said. "It saves you time to do it yourself."

"And the company from having to pay wages, health care, pension, and—"

"It's fucking Walmart! They don't give their employees shit!"

The woman at the podium shot Horace a venomous look. I grabbed the bag of clothes and made my way toward the exit. Horace followed me. I didn't want to be in the store any longer. Horace's behavior was going to get us severely injured by some xenophobic locals or involved with law enforcement that didn't care for outsiders. Being in public with him was like tending to an unruly child. The episode was embarrassing and now he goaded a threat of bodily harm from spectators.

We made it to the car without any more incidents. Horace stopped by a Wendy's and bought several sandwiches for a dollar apiece before heading back to the hotel.

16

Horace spent an exorbitant amount of time in the bathroom preparing for the ceremony. While he groomed himself I flipped through TV channels. I settled on a marathon of a show called *The Forensic Files*.

An hour and a half before the ceremony Horace exited the bathroom. He wore the lavender shirt tucked into the pleated pants and had already knotted his tie. He retrieved the fedora he'd purchased and perched it on his head. He stood in front of the full-length mirror and tilted the hat forward.

He said, "What do you think?" He turned to me and held out his arms.

"You're trying too hard and you look ludicrous."

"You wouldn't know style if it bit you in the arse!"

I turned my attention back to the television. "Okay."

He waved at me dismissively and went to the mini fridge. He grabbed the bag of sandwiches and held it up and said, "Do you want any?"

"Sure."

Horace dumped the bag's contents on the dresser by the television and proceeded to place all the wrapped burgers into the small microwave. He set the timer to five minutes.

I said, "That's too much time."

"There are six of them. That's less than a minute each."

"I don't think it works that way."

"You're a fashion expert and a microwave scientist?!"

I didn't reply. I turned my attention to the television program. He stood in front of the microwave with his arms crossed and watched the food rotate. Once the microwave was done he opened the door and picked up one of the burgers. He immediately spun and simultaneously yelped, tossing the sandwich on my bed. The wrapping came undone upon impact and the burger tumbled onto the duvet. Ketchup smeared on my bed.

"Damn it, Horace!"

He shook his wounded hand and shouted, "That motherfucker is nuclear hot!"

I got up, retrieved some toilet tissue, and cleaned up the mess. Horace carefully removed the remaining burgers from the microwave by scooting them onto the flattened sack they came in. He set them on the desk. We waited a few minutes for them to cool before attempting to eat them.

Once we were finished eating Horace opened the window and proceeded to chain smoke cigarettes until a quarter till eight. At that time he decided we should go to the lobby a few minutes early. I grabbed the box of cassettes and we took the elevator down.

The flimsy sign at the lobby had been changed. It now said the lobby eating area was closed for a ceremony and would re-open shortly.

We entered the side room area and found someone had rearranged the tables and chairs to create a clearing in the center. There were two rows of five chairs and an empty table in front of the chairs. Two women sat on opposite ends of the front row. One of the women was thin and decked out in bohemian apparel and oversized sunglasses. She had dreadlocks in need of maintenance. The other woman was pudgy and looked as though a child dressed her: a bra as a shirt, an ill fitted blazer made out of denim material, giant black framed glasses, unbrushed and stringy blond hair, and jeans so tight she looked like a biscuit popped out of a can.

In the back row an obese man in a faded black T-shirt and worn sweatpants sat alone behind the hippie girl with his arms folded over his chest. He'd pulled his chair away from the others in the row to make room for his size. He ogled the women in the front row, favoring the girl in the denim blazer since she was scantily clad.

Horace led the way and sat in the back row behind the girl in the blazer, allowing me to have the seat on the end. I set the box of cassettes beside me on the floor. The other three turned to size us up. None of us offered an introduction and eventually the two women turned to face the front again. The woman in the denim jacket produced a phone and began playing with it. Two hotel employees at the check-in desk across the hall laughed and I assumed they were ridiculing us.

An excruciating amount of time elapsed. Horace pulled his phone from his pocket and diddled with it. After a couple of minutes he tapped my arm and held the phone for me to see a photo of the girl in front of us. In the photo she appeared drunk.

I said, "Where'd you get that?"

The other three made slight movements and I was aware they were listening to our conversation but pretending not to care.

Horace pushed a couple of buttons on his phone and began to type. When he was done he showed me a yellow screen with lines on it to look like a yellow legal note pad. He'd typed: I saw her Facebook profile over her shoulder and searched her.

I gave him a disgusted look. He touched something on his screen and a keyboard materialized. He handed me his phone. I typed but other letters started to appear on the screen. I didn't know how to correct my mistakes and gave up. My message ended up reading: serial killer would say fuck old fart stalker. Horace read the sentence and laughed. The other three flinched at his outburst.

A man in his thirties wearing a baggy brown suit appeared. His suit looked as though it had been hanging on a thrift store rack thirty minutes prior. He held a cheap gold trophy. His haircut was clearly self-administered. He sat the trophy on the table and pulled a piece of paper from his inside blazer pocket.

He unfolded the paper, cleared his throat, and read, "Hello, everyone. Thank you for attending Dr. Wiwi's Sales Award ceremony. I know some of you have traveled far distances to be here today."

The obese man interrupted. "I live in town."

We all side glanced the obese guy. The man in the brown suit laughed nervously and continued his speech. My attention was distracted from the speech by Horace. He leaned close to me and the brim of his hat hit me in the temple. He showed me his phone. He'd typed 'rude fat fuck'. Once I acknowledged his message he typed 'he doesn't sound British' and pointed at the man speaking. I nodded and recoiled from Horace. He reeked of booze. I tried to pay attention to the guy in the suit but his speech reminded me of the dull meetings I was forced to attend at my office job. I never gave a shit about how much money the company was or wasn't making. All I cared about was my paycheck. And some would lead you to believe you should give a fuck because if the company didn't make money their need for you as an employee could be cut and you wouldn't make money either. The way I saw it the numbers and running the business should be left to the accountant and owner, not the peons.

Horace continued to screw with his phone. I wanted to elbow him and make him pay attention. After all, it was his idea to come to the damn thing in this awful town. I would've been content at home, not spending money, wallowing in self-pity, and waiting for Social Security to kick in or sweet death to take me. Whichever came first if I didn't prompt the latter at my own hand.

A thought struck me. I hadn't thought about Beverly since leaving the house without prompting. As much as it pained me to admit, Horace was right. The only way to keep all of the evil shit out of your head and stay sane was to keep going. You *had* to keep busy. If the world stopped . . . if the people of the world stopped everything they were doing and sat down in a quiet room by themselves with no music or television or Internet or phones and were forced to examine the content of their thoughts the majority of them would realize they were depressed. Or they would see their situation was depressing or life sucked and there wasn't much they could do to remedy the situation. Or there wasn't anything they were willing to do to remedy the situation. If you were poor you were poor. You might be able to work hard and climb one rung of the social status ladder but you would always have the poor mentality. A person would never be rich by wishing they would become rich. They could become rich by sheer luck. No one strived for much, only enough. And only enough was the best you could hope for.

Beverly was dead. There was no changing that. I was fucking sad because of it. The best I could hope for was enough mental capacity to deal with it. The alternative was—as with anything—death. Bad things happened every day to everyone. You could try to change what was making you unhappy but in the end you would end up unhappy because nothing changes. The best you could do was change your situation by removing what made you unhappy.

The man in the brown suit interrupted my train of thought. He shouted, "And now for the moment you all have been waiting for!" He reached into his blazer and produced an envelope.

The man in our row scooted in his chair to sit up straighter. It was apparent he either thought he was the winner or he desperately wanted to be the winner. Regardless, his wishes were pathetic and sad if your major goal in life was to beat three other sad fucks and gain a shitty plastic gold trophy.

The man in the brown suit opened the envelope and said, "The winner for this year's Best in Sales is . . ." He paused for effect.

"Come on," the obese man muttered.

"Sophia Rutherford," he said. He squinted at the card and said, "Also known as Moon Journey?"

The obese man made a disgusted sound. He rocked a couple of times in his chair to shift his weight and get to his feet. The woman dressed in bohemian garb snapped to attention and stood. The woman in the blazer watched the obese man struggle to stand. The large man immediately made his way to the front doors of the hotel and exited. Sophia or Moon Journey or whoever approached the man in the brown suit.

The announcer lifted the trophy off the table and extended it to the woman. She took it awkwardly and the man asked her if she wanted to say a few words. She shook her head and gave a small laugh.

The man stared at her for an awkward second and said, "Okay. This concludes our ceremony. I want to thank you all for coming."

Moon Journey dug into a bottomless pocket hand sewn on the front of her skirt and retrieved a pack of cigarettes. She listlessly walked toward the front doors.

The woman in the blazer sat unmoving. She watched the man in the brown suit as he began to rearrange the tables and chairs. She appeared as if she expected more to happen.

Horace stood and said, "That was pointless."

I stood and lifted the box of cassettes. Horace's eyes brightened. He'd completely forgotten about the tapes. I approached the man who was too involved with his task to realize I was trying to get his attention.

I said, "Excuse me."

Horace stood a couple of steps away. The man stopped dragging a table across the carpet and turned to me. I dropped the box of cassettes too roughly on the table he'd been moving.

Horace said, "Are you Dr. Wiwi?"

"Horace," I said. I motioned for him to be quiet. "Please." I turned my attention back to the man.

The man said, "My name's Chuck. There's no Dr. Wiwi. He's a fictitious spokesperson for the company. Like Colonel Sanders."

"Colonel Sanders was real," Horace said.

I waved impatiently for Horace to leave. "Would you go smoke or something?"

Chuck said, "Can I help you? I don't have a lot of time. I need to put the furniture back and clean up."

"Yeah," I said. "I quit." I pointed at the box on the table. "I'm returning what merchandise I have."

"Okay," Chuck said. He wasn't fazed by my announcement.

Horace said, "If there's no Dr. Wiwi whose voice is on the tapes?"

Chuck said, "It's a narrator I paid."

I said, "Do you need my name or information? Since I'm quitting?"

Chuck shrugged nonchalantly. "Not really."

"And you're going to remove my phone number from the advertisements."

"I don't deal with that."

"Who does? I want to talk to them."

"Look," Chuck said. "I'm very busy. Now if you'd—"

Horace shouted, "Punch him in the cocksucker!"

"What?!" I said. "No!"

Chuck held up his hands in surrender and took a step back. "Hey, I don't want any trouble—"

Horace said, "If he won't take your number off the list, punch him!" Horace pointed at Chuck. "There's a no call list and it's the law!"

"Jesus," I said, "that's not what the no call list means." I addressed Chuck. "I'm sorry. My friend is senile. He gets angry and confused sometimes."

"Fuck you!" Horace shouted. "I'm not senile! Punch the snotnose prick in the balls!"

Chuck covered his testicles. "Please don't punch me."

"I'm not punching him!" I shouted at Horace.

Chuck took another step back and looked toward the check-in desk for help. He maneuvered himself to put the table between us.

The hotel employee at the desk called, "Do we need to call the police?"

"No," I said. I grabbed Horace's arm and spun him around. I dragged him toward the entrance. "We're leaving. I'm sorry."

The sky was darkening outside and no one was around. We walked across the carport to the smoking area with the bench. I was going to sit on the bench but someone had spilled something on it.

Horace pointed at the front entrance and shouted, "Fuck that guy!" He produced a cigarette and lit it.

I said, "Would you stop trying to fight people?"

He blew the smoke as he spoke. "Someone's gotta show them they're assholes."

"Beating people up proves they're assholes?"

"Yeah."

"I think it proves you're an asshole."

He stepped close, putting his face close to mine. "You don't know shit!"

I lifted my hand in front of his face and hit the brim of his hat, knocking it off his head. His reflexes were delayed by the alcohol and I took the opportunity to stomp on the hat.

"You look like an asshole with that hat!" I shouted.

Horace yelled. I kept my foot planted on the hat and he tried to push me over. I took a few steps to keep from falling. He retrieved his flattened hat and almost fell in the process. He tucked the cigarette between his lips and tried to remold the hat. Nothing he did reshaped it correctly and the hat would need to be replaced. He put the hat on his head and pulled a flask from the front pocket of his deep pleated pants.

I said, "Now you look homeless."

He ignored me.

I nodded toward the flask. "That explains a lot."

"It's just scotch."

"Exactly."

Moon Journey stepped around the side of the building with a lit cigarette. She still held the trophy. She shyly waved at us. Her oversized sunglasses hid her expression except for her lightly wrinkled smile.

"Congratulations," I said.

She approached us. "It's nothing." She held the trophy toward me. "It's like . . . made out of plastic or something. I bet they got it out of one of those crane machines filled with stuffed animals, you know?"

I took the trophy and inspected it. In the square where an engraved announcement should've been there was a flimsy gold sticker with '#1' printed on it. I chuckled and handed it back to her.

I said, "I told Chuck I quit."

"Who's Chuck?" she said.

Horace said, "The douchebag in the suit." He took a drink from the flask.

"What are you drinking?" she asked.

"Scotch." He offered her the flask.

She waved it away. "No thanks. You guys want to get high?"

I opened my mouth to tell her thanks for offering but no thank you. Horace beat me to the punch.

"Sure!" he said enthusiastically.

I shot Horace a wide-eyed glance. I briefly debated protesting but I didn't want to offend Moon Journey. And I didn't want to look like an old fart fuddy-duddy. My second thought was to excuse myself in a polite way and allow them to do what they wanted since they were adults and could handle themselves. I personally didn't have anything against smoking pot—if it was what she was insinuating—but I'd been so far removed from marijuana I didn't think it would be a good idea. I didn't know how old Moon Journey was but I put her at around forty. She hadn't known the days of war and protests and real hippies who smoked pot and took acid and fought against the government and ultimately became so consumed with doing drugs they lost the plot and chose to get high all the time instead. I was no stranger to marijuana. Especially once I was drafted and returned from Vietnam a year later with a superficial bullet wound in my thigh and a Purple Heart. My leg wasn't the only thing fucked up when I got home and pot did wonders for the pain—emotionally and psychologically. Once I'd met Beverly my priorities drastically changed. Money was for taking care of your family, not for rolling up and smoking. Beverly told me she wouldn't marry me unless I stopped. And I did. For her.

Horace and Moon Journey stared at me expectantly for a reply. Horace capped his flask and slid it back into his front pocket.

I said, "What do I have to lose?"

Moon Journey led us to her green and white Volkswagen Bus. There were orange curtains on the back windows and all of them were closed. Moon Journey opened the back doors and the overwhelming stench of marijuana wafted out. There were no seats in the back of the van but a mattress. A man with long dirty blond hair lay on the far side of the mattress, asleep. He was barefoot and shirtless, which exposed his beer gut. He wore a pair of bellbottom jeans or what the grandkids renamed flares. The man didn't stir as Moon Journey entered the van.

Once Moon Journey was in the van she turned to us. "Don't worry about waking Astral Plane. He spent all day searching for his spirit animal with some guidance."

Moon Journey stepped to the back of the van and flipped a switch on a sickly yellow overhead light. Horace and I entered. She sat with her legs crossed in the lotus position on the floor, surrounded by dirty clothes and discarded food wrappers. I knew I was too old to get into that position. Horace sat on the hump covering the tire. I had no other option than to sit beside the sleeping man. I struggled to cross my legs but my bruised knee was too stiff. The most comfortable position I could obtain was to lie beside the man on the mattress. Moon Journey tossed her award in the pile of clothes. She retrieved a brown pouch made of suede and unzipped it. She pulled a green glass pipe and a clear and silver Ziploc bag from within the pouch.

I said, "That's a strange baggy."

She lifted the plastic bag. "This?"

"Yeah," I said. "I've only ever seen pot in cheap plastic sandwich bags."

"Because this is legal."

Horace said, "Get the fuck out."

"I'm not kidding. I live in Oregon. Recreational pot is legal there."

"But not here," I said.

She removed her sunglasses. In the faint light filtering through the orange curtains combined with the overhead light her eyes appeared dark brown. She had a smattering of wrinkles around her eyes when she smiled.

"Probably not," she responded.

Horace extended his hand to her. "Can I see it?"

"Sure." She handed him the bag.

He inspected it for a few seconds and passed it to me. There was a label on the front with strange names and numbers. I opened the bag and smelled it. The stench was a lot stronger than what I remembered.

Moon Journey said, "It's sativa."

I handed the bag back to her. Astral Plane gave a small snort in his sleep. The sound from his close proximity startled me. He smacked his lips but did not wake.

Horace said, "What's sativas?"

She said, "There are two different kinds. Sativa and indica."

I said, "There was only one kind when I smoked it. It was called pot."

She laughed. "There are a million different kinds. I prefer the sativa because they give you energy." She pointed at Astral Plane. "As you can tell he likes the indica. That stuff turns me into a zombie. I don't like it." She pointed her chin at him and pinched off small pieces of the marijuana and stuffed it into the glass pipe. "Sativas are horrible for him. They make him super paranoid." She finished stuffing the pipe and handed it and a lighter she found on the floor to me. "I'll let you have the honors."

I propped myself up on my elbows and took the pipe and lighter. I had always smoked joints. The pipe felt strange in my hands. I lit the lighter, ran it over the marijuana, and sucked at the same time.

"Oh," she said, "it has a carburetor." She indicated the small hole on the side of the pipe. "Hold your finger over the hole and take your finger off once the pipe is full of smoke."

I attempted to light the pipe a second time and succeeded. I assumed I would end up coughing like crazy since it had been a lifetime since the last time I'd smoked pot but I didn't. The smoke was smooth and tasted like burnt peanuts. Horace laughed at me and took the pipe and lighter from me. The pipe went around a couple of times before its effect hit me. The sensation was like being hit with a semi-truck. My first thought was I did not need to smoke any more.

I waved the pipe away when Moon Journey tried to pass it to me again. "I'm good," I said. I lay down beside Astral Plane and watched the other two pass the pipe back and forth.

Astral Plane rolled over to face the wall of the van as the others finished smoking the contents of the pipe. Horace and Moon Journey struck up a conversation about gardening. She explained the mysteries of some of her troublesome tomato plants and how they didn't taste as sweet this year as they had in the past. She and Horace's conversation was a game of tennis. She spoke. He spoke. The ball of words bounced back and forth. I tried to be polite and ask her questions to keep engaged. I don't know why but I always tried to act sober whenever I was inebriated or high.

I began to pick out key words in their conversation and their pronunciation of those key words. The more they spoke the more those particular words became prominent. One of the two would mutter 'hmm' while the other was speaking. After a sentence was completed the other would respond with 'yeah'. The next sentence would be spoken and the other would confirm their statement with an 'uh-huh'. When either of them had a revelation to what the speaker was saying they would say 'okay'. These four words, 'hmm, yeah, uh-huh, okay' slowly became the only four words I could understand coming from their mouths. Their conversation became a new language of the four words only they could understand.

My heart raced and I began to panic. I didn't think they would be able to understand me if I spoke since I didn't speak their language. I told myself I was high and it was something I was imagining. I forced myself to focus on what each of them said. I studied the shapes their lips formed and I was able to briefly break through the language barrier and hear what they were really saying. One brief intrusion into their conversation informed me they were talking about feeding beer to slugs to keep them out of the vegetable garden.

The panic of my inability to understand them made me want to get away from them. My thoughts became consumed with the idea I needed to go back to the hotel room.

Whatever was happening to me never happened before when I smoked pot. An imaginary force of flight engulfed me and in my mind's eye the force materialized. An arrow emerged from my body and pointed in the direction either it or I wanted to go. It beckoned me to leave the van. The arrow grew and extended toward the hotel room. I thought of the arrow and the direction it wanted me to go as an omen. A creeping sense of tragedy crawled up my spine. I knew something bad was about to happen to me if I didn't follow it.

I didn't want the other two to know I couldn't understand them and there was a force telling me to leave them. I made small movements to sit up. Each movement was broken into a million steps and I was afraid to perform them all at once. If I didn't break the momentum of sitting into slow steps I would be compelled to bolt up in a flash, throw open the van door, and sprint into the hotel in a screaming panic. First I propped myself up on my elbows. Then I sat up. Then I rearranged myself so I sat on my haunches.

The two talked in code to each other and ignored me.

Horace said, "Hmm, yeah, uh-huh, okay."

Moon Journey said, "Hmm, yeah, uh-huh, okay."

I said, "Guys, I'm gonna go lay down."

Moon Journey's chant altered. She said, "Oh. Are you okay?"

There was one of the words. She said the word 'okay'. I heard the chant now without either one of them speaking.

hmm, yeah, uh-huh, okay, hmm, yeah, uh-huh, okay, hmm, yeah, uh-huh, okay

I said, "I'm fine. Just tired."

I didn't want to say 'yeah'. I was afraid I might become

consumed with the chant looping through my brain if I
repeated one of their words. I said a quick goodbye and
exited the van. Horace stayed behind. It had grown dark.
Even outside the van I could hear the chant and the voices
turned into something alien and musical. My heart raced
and I could feel a thin layer of sweat forming all over my
body. I walked to the front of the hotel. My footfalls
sounded like gun blasts in the quiet night and I wondered
how long I was in Moon Journey's van. The chanting fell
into the rhythm of my pace.

hmm, yeah, uh-huh, okay, hmm, yeah, uh-huh, okay, hmm,
yeah, uh-huh, okay

I avoided eye contact with the hotel employee behind
the check-in desk and rushed toward the elevator. The elevator took an obscene amount of time to appear. I repeatedly hit the button and gasped for breath while my heart
hammered. I worried I was in the beginning stages of a
heart attack when my chest wouldn't hurt or I wouldn't
feel any pain because of the pot. The dilemma of calling
an ambulance crossed my mind when the elevator doors
opened. I rode to our floor with my brain in chaos. I exited the elevator in a run and fumbled with the key to open
the door. Once I was in the room I crawled into bed and
pulled the covers over my head as if I were a child hiding
from an imaginary monster in the dark.

Was I having a heart attack? Should I tell the EMS per-
sonnel I was high if I called them? Would I go to jail?
What if I wasn't having a heart attack and I was having a
panic attack brought on by smoking pot? Would I still go
to jail? Would Horace ridicule me for being a pussy?

I decided I was having an episode of some sort and
there was nothing a doctor could do for me. I decided I

was dying. I was going to die in a shitty Holiday Inn in Covington, Virginia. Horace would try to wake me in the morning. I would be long gone and cold and stiff. I guess that was a better way of going than how I planned my death earlier. The best thing for me was to relax. Enjoy the ride. Let go.

Starting with my toes I tried to relax. I told each muscle to stop constricting until I reached the top of my head. It was a slow going process but I managed to make my body into nothingness.

Next I worked on my breathing. I took deep breaths and let them out slowly, trying to slow my racing heart. My heart obeyed and grew sluggish. My breaths became shallower and shallower. My body shifted slightly and began to pull into itself. The bed felt nonexistent and I was sucked backward. Everything around me disappeared and I was left only with the sensation of traveling in reverse. My life was in rewind until I was sucked into my mother's womb and from there I was pulled backward through the universe. Thin white lights streaked by as I soared past the stars. The force that compelled me to come to this room was pulling my soul through time and space and now everything was slowing down and I knew I was approaching a void. I became weightless and nothing. The backward momentum of the journey left me drifting aimlessly in nothingness. And almost imperceptibly, I came to a stop. The world came to a stop. The universe came to a stop. Frozen in time. Frozen in nothingness. Frozen before the existence of anything.

A wet smacking sound interrupted the annihilation of the universe. I forced my eyes open. A bright square of light penetrated through the threads of fabric. The blanket was still pulled over my head and Horace had turned on the television. The smacking sound persisted. I pulled the blanket from my head. My drug fogged brain didn't take too long to process what was happening.

The room was dark except for the television. Horace and Moon Journey were on Horace's bed. She was on all fours with her skirt hitched over her hips and her panties pulled down to her knees. Horace was behind her. His pants were undone and pulled down just far enough to fuck her. Both of them wore blank expressions and stared at the television. They were enthralled by the program. The volume wasn't on but the screen displayed horrific images of bloodied body parts and a reenacted scene of murder and a man placing a dead woman in the trunk of a vehicle. The bottom right corner of the screen displayed the logo for *The Forensic Files*.

I slipped out of bed. The marijuana screwed with my equilibrium and I tried not to fall or make noise or be noticed by the two. I expected Horace and Moon Journey to realize I was awake and stop or become embarrassed. But they didn't. They continued fucking and watching the scenes of senseless murder being replayed on the screen.

I gathered my bag at the foot of the bed and went into the bathroom. I urinated, brushed my teeth, drank handfuls of water from the tap, washed my face, shaved, and exited the bathroom. Horace and Moon Journey continued to fuck. I tossed my key card on my bed and exited the room with my bag in tow. The sensation of waking up high was disorienting. My thoughts came slow and my body was sluggish and resistant to comply with my thoughts.

There was no employee behind the check-in desk. I

rang the service bell a couple of times. Eventually a groggy girl in her twenties with disheveled brown hair finally appeared. She looked panicked and confused. I was sure she was sleeping in the back but I made no mention of it. I didn't want to draw too much attention to myself.

I said, "Where's the nearest bus station?"

"Uh." She rubbed the sleep from one eye. "I don't think there's a bus station in Covington. I don't know though. I've never taken a bus. Only flew."

"Where's the airport?"

"The closest one is in Roanoke. About an hour and a half away."

"How can I get there if I don't have a car?"

She shrugged. Her eyes skimmed the desk's surface as if the answer was engraved on it somewhere.

I said, "Why does Covington exist?"

Straight-faced she said, "I ask myself the same question all the time." She suddenly perked up. "Oh! I know. You can rent a car. Enterprise. You know? They'll pick you up. They'll come get you if you rent from them. You could drive to Roanoke and return the car at the airport."

I said, "Thank you. Can you find their number for me and can I use your phone?"

17

Life wasn't that simple. The car rental company was closed until nine A.M. Monday. It was three A.M. on Sunday and I had to kill some time. I refused to go back to Horace's room. I was done with him. I needed to be alone. I needed to sober up. The pot Moon Journey gave me was nothing like the marijuana I smoked long ago. The experience was like nothing before and I wondered if she hadn't slipped me acid. I've never had audio and visual hallucinations from marijuana. And I didn't think the state of Oregon would allow such a thing to be sold.

The desk clerk wrote down the number for the car rental agency and I left the Holiday Inn. In our comings and goings I'd spotted another chain motel within a stone's throw. There was a rundown motel right beside the Holiday Inn with a neon motel sign on the roof but it looked like something Norman Bates would live in. Beyond the Norman Bates motel was a better option. I walked through the parking lot in the middle of the night and checked into the other motel and was forced to pay for two nights.

The room at the other hotel was dismal. The carpets were stained. The bathtub had a ring of black filth. The air didn't work. And I was too tired and high to care. I slept until noon and walked to McDonald's to eat breakfast. I watched television to kill time.

Eventually I sobered but the high was replaced with a hollowness that frightened me. I left again to eat supper and before going to bed I set my alarm for nine in the morning. When the alarm sounded I called the car rental agency. I ate breakfast from the hotel smorgasbord, pilfering a couple of bananas for the road.

The car rental company did as advertised. They came and got me. They took me to their office to sign some paperwork and I was on my way.

My first stop was a gas station. Apparently a great bit of time had passed since my last road trip. Maps were now obsolete. The greasy-haired man at the gas station told me to use my phone or GPS. I told him I didn't own a phone and I didn't pay the extra money for the GPS because I didn't know how to operate one. He sighed heavily and diddled with his phone for a few minutes and jotted down the directions on a piece of paper.

My brain was on empty and in autopilot mode. I didn't want to think about what was at home. I didn't know why I was going home. There wasn't anything left for me there. But I followed the man's directions to the airport car return.

The airline employees were kinder. I waited in a lounge area into the night until a seat was open for a flight to Dayton, Ohio. When I touched down the sun was beginning to rise. I shilled out too much money for a taxi to take me to Yellow Springs instead of fucking with Dayton's terrible bus system that would've add another two hours to my trip.

When I arrived at the house I started to insert the key into the lock but stopped short. I dropped my bag under the carport and took off walking instead. The day was nice. You could tell it was going to be hot. The dew had already evaporated and the air was heavy with humidity. The sky was clear and the sun beat down on me as I walked down the road toward the cemetery.

The cemetery was a quarter of a mile from the house Beverly and I spent most of our marriage in. She had chosen the house for the yard. I still remembered the beam in her eyes when she told me it would be perfect for the children we didn't have at the time. Nathan was born a year after we moved in. Tara came along a couple of years later and everything was complete. They attended the local school. We built a life. The kids grew into adults and moved on to create their own lives. And then Beverly died. I couldn't find one good reason why I should still be here.

The grass of the cemetery was slightly overgrown and songbirds serenaded my first walk to Beverly's grave. I stopped in front of the tombstone I'd never laid my eyes on. I had avoided her grave. Chiseled into the stone and irreversible was Beverly's full name, the date she was born, and the date she left me. I purposely avoided this place once she'd been laid to rest. I attempted several times to force myself to come here and make the whole nightmare real. But the notion of visiting her grave was completely demolished once the funeral home informed me her grave marker was set. Because right there beside her name and the two simple dates summing up her life to anyone who happened to walk by was my name and the date I was born. I stared at the blank space where my expiration date would be chiseled. The end. Everything about me would exist between those dates. This stone would be the only thing in existence proving I had once been a sack of living and breathing tissue that moved from one place to another with thoughts and feelings and dreams and goals and love and hate. The date would be as concrete as death itself.

I didn't speak to Beverly. The thought of talking to her aloud was ridiculous to me. I knew other people spoke to their loved ones in a cemetery but it all felt moot to me. Beverly wasn't here. It didn't mean she wasn't here physically but roamed somewhere spiritually. No. She wasn't here. She wasn't in a fantastic afterlife either. Beverly was dead. All that was left was her dead and rotting flesh that would eventually disintegrate altogether.

I lay down on the grass under the engraving with my name and birthdate. The ground over Beverly's grave consisted of lumpy mud clumps and the grass was patchy. I ran my hand through the grass as if it were her hair and became still.

If anyone would've been in the graveyard they might have thought me crazy. I shut my eyes and focused on the warmth from the sun's rays. I thought, *Maybe I should lie here until I'm absorbed into the earth. Or maybe I'll get up in couple of minutes and walk home.* Who knew what the next few minutes would bring.

Other Atlatl Press Titles

The Beard by Andersen Prunty

They Had Goat Heads by D. Harlan Wilson

Losing the Light by Brian Cartwright

Fuckness by Andersen Prunty

Mastodon Farm by Mike Kleine

Fill the Grand Canyon and Live Forever by Andersen Prunty

Death Metal Epic (Book 1: The Inverted Katabasis) by Dean Swinford

Thanks For Ruining My Life by C.V. Hunt

Drinking Until Morning by Justin Grimbol

Arafat Mountain by Mike Kleine

Hard Bodies by Justin Grimbol

Squirm With Me by Andersen Prunty

Made in the USA
Columbia, SC
26 June 2020